Shelby let her breath out with a whoosh.

Noiselessly, she turned the doorknob and opened the door. The room was totally dark, but she could hear hoarse snoring from the direction of the couch. Creeping along with her hand gliding on the wall, she made her way toward the door. Her progress seemed perilously slow. She felt along with her feet, and finally she was at the doorway to the outer room.

The snore behind her paused, and her mouth went dry. The snoring resumed, and her shoulders relaxed. Inching forward again, she made her way to the door. Her hand went to the doorknob. It was locked. Hunching her shoulders, she felt for the lock. There it was. She slid it back, and it made a grinding noise. Pausing, she listened for sound from the other room, but all she heard was the snoring. She eased the door open.

The cool air cleared her head. She looked at the small knife in her hand. At the time she found it, it had seemed very inadequate. But God had known what she needed. He wouldn't let her down now. Rushing through the quiet and deserted streets, her breath whistled through _____ h. She would make it to the b___ __

$2.50

COLLEEN COBLE and her husband, David, have been married twenty-nine years this October. They have two great kids, David Jr. and Kara. Though Colleen is still waiting for grandchildren, she makes do with the nursery inhabitants at New Life Baptist Church. She is very active at her church where she sings and helps her husband with a young adult Sunday School class. She enjoys the various activities with the class including horseback riding (she needs a stool to mount) and canoeing (she tips the canoe every time). She is also an espresso nut and loves iced lattes. A voracious reader herself, Colleen began pursuing her lifelong dream when a younger brother, Randy Rhoads, was killed by lightning when she was thirty-eight. *Love Ahoy* is her sixth novel. Watch for her novellas also in your local Christian bookstore.

Books by Coleen Coble

Don't miss out on any of our super romances. Write to us at the following address for information on our newest releases and club membership.

Heartsong Presents Readers' Service
PO Box 721
Uhrichsville, OH 44683

Love
Ahoy

Colleen Coble

Heartsong Presents

For all the Fordyce family, my "other family" in Arizona, and especially for Scarlet the Precious, the family's Yorkshire terrier who thinks she is a real girl.

A note from the author:
I love to hear from my readers! You may correspond with me by writing: **Colleen Coble**
Author Relations
PO Box 719
Uhrichsville, OH 44683

ISBN 1-58660-203-9

LOVE AHOY

Scripture taken from the HOLY BIBLE: NEW INTERNATIONAL VERSION®. NIV®. Copyright © 1973, 1978, 1984 by International Bible Society. Used by permission of Zondervan Publishing House.

Cover illustration by Ron Hall.

PRINTED IN THE U.S.A.

one

Shelby West paused her flipping of pages to stare at an ad for a cruise. A long-limbed model, her glorious mane of blond hair whipping in the wind, sailed on the azure bay of some tropical paradise. Shelby sighed and hunched in her chair. Why had she chosen a career in advertising? It just made her feel inadequate. At six-feet-one-inch tall, she towered over the average man and made him feel anything but masculine.

Shelby sighed again. Maybe her size was why she was stuck here in this eight-foot-square cubicle. Instead of feeling the sea breeze in her face, she breathed the ozone of the copier and the stale smoke of the men at the counter. She glanced again at the sailboat and shuddered—not that she'd ever dare to sail. She was terrified of the water.

She straightened the line of her jacket and jotted down some ideas for the new ad campaign for Lamar Foods. Anything to keep from dwelling on the differences between her and the beautiful women in the magazines. Sometimes she longed to wear feminine, fluffy clothes like she saw other women wear. The one time she'd worn something with ruffles to the office, the men hadn't noticed and the women had eyed her under their lashes like she was a bug in a laboratory. After that, she stuck with her usual tailored business suits and combed-back hair neatly confined in a bun.

Her phone rang, and she picked it up. There was an excited squawk through the headset, and she winced. "Calm down, Mom. I'm not deaf."

Her mother toned down her voice. "Shelby, the most amazing thing has happened! You're an heiress!"

An heiress? Shelby couldn't stop the bark of laughter that escaped. "Were you napping, Mom?" Her mother must have been dreaming, though she wasn't usually so off-center. Her rampant arthritis left her depressed most of the time, not given to flights of fancy.

"I'm serious, Shelby! I knew he was fairly well off, but I never dreamed he'd leave his holdings to you. I always assumed Palmer would inherit."

Palmer. The name sounded familiar, but Shelby's bewilderment grew as her mother droned on. Her thoughts raced through the list of her relatives and loved ones. She wouldn't willingly lose any of them, but then, none of the ones she could think of had any money. She cleared her throat and broke into her mother's excited ramblings. "Who died, Mom?"

"My Uncle Lloyd out in California. You remember him, don't you, Shelby?"

Shelby nodded uncertainly, then remembered her mother couldn't see her. "I think so. Wasn't he the tall, gaunt man with a nearly bald head and watery blue eyes who rambled on about knots and fathoms and halyards?" She thought she'd met him at her grandparents' sixtieth wedding anniversary party five years ago. "The one with the boat charter business?" The one who chided her for her refusal to face her fear of water. She'd told him about nearly drowning, but that hadn't mattered to him. He had wanted her to come on a cruise with him, but she'd refused.

Her gaze traveled back to the model in the magazine, and the pulse in her throat jumped. Her yearning for adventure had grown nearly overpowering lately. She'd come to accept the fact that men weren't interested in a woman who towered over them and looked like a female Viking warrior, but staying single didn't preclude adventure and fun. . . .

But unfortunately, it had to be a mistake. "Mom, you must have it wrong. Why would he leave me anything? I only met him that one time."

"I don't really know, Darling. But his lawyer called and said you needed to get out there for the reading of the will." Her mother's voice was high and excited.

"Where?" Shelby's thoughts skittered, but she managed to corral them.

"Sandy Cove, California. About fifty miles from San Francisco. The reading of the will is next Monday." She dropped her voice to a confidential whisper. "The lawyer said it was a lot of money."

Shelby's fingers tightened, and the pencil in her fingers snapped. "He was probably bankrupt," she said. That was the way her luck ran. She bit her lip. Here she was thinking about possessions, when the poor man was dead and in either heaven or hell. She vaguely remembered talking to him about God. He had told her he became a Christian when he was in his thirties. The tightness in her chest eased. But why would he leave her anything? She had barely known him.

She said good-bye to her mother and hung up the phone. Her thoughts buzzed with questions, and she went to see her supervisor to arrange her vacation. In spite of her mother's assurances, she couldn't afford to just quit. This sounded too good to be true and probably was. But she couldn't squelch the thrill of excitement; at least she would get away for a few weeks.

The next two days Shelby packed, arranged for a friend to water her plants, and made travel arrangements. She cleaned the apartment, told her friends at New Life Baptist Church about her plans, and spent a lot of time staring out the window. The cold weather of Wabash, Indiana, would soon be replaced by blue skies and sunshine, white-capped waves and the scent of the sea. It was hard for Shelby to even comprehend. She couldn't imagine why her uncle had done this. Maybe California held the answer to that question.

Monday morning, her mother took her to the Fort Wayne airport and parked at the curb by the gate. Her mother shot a glare of disdain at Scarlet, Shelby's one-year-old Yorkshire terrier. "I don't know why you have to take that dog," she said. "She'll yap the entire trip. And you really should have left yesterday. I would have been fine. As it is, you'll have to hurry to make your appointment."

The red bow on Scarlet's head was askew, and Shelby's mother straightened it. Scarlet rewarded her with a lick, and her mother's grim expression softened. Shelby hid a grin. Bonnie West might fool herself into thinking she hated all dogs, but her daughter knew better. Scarlet could weasel her way into the stoniest heart.

"I wish you'd let me go with you," her mother said fretfully.

Shelby sighed, then reminded her mother, "You have

that doctor's appointment next week, and Robert is coming for a visit next weekend. If I'm spending the money on a ticket, I might as well stay a bit and enjoy my time off. And if Uncle Lloyd really did leave me anything, I'll need to see to the details."

Shelby had known she needed to make the trip alone because her mother simply wasn't up to a trip that might turn out to be a vanishing pot of gold at the end of a nonexistent rainbow. If anything came of this so-called inheritance, her mother could come out later. And maybe the weather would help her mom. Shelby was afraid to even hope for that.

"I suppose you're right," her mother responded as she brushed Shelby's hair back from her face. "I just worry about you. All you seem to care about is your job." She smoothed Shelby's already controlled hair. "And you never date. It's as if you are warning men off with your lovely hair plastered to your head and those mannish clothes. I never see you in clothes that show off what a beautiful young woman you are."

Shelby managed a smile. "Only *you* would think I am beautiful," she said. "Men don't want a woman who towers over them." She popped Scarlet into the pet carrier. "It's about boarding time. You don't try to walk with me to the gate. I'll call when I get there." She leaned across the seat and kissed her mother then opened the door and grabbed her suitcase from the back seat.

"Be careful in San Francisco," her mother called after her.

The confident wave she gave her mother hid the trepidation that churned her stomach. What on earth was she doing? Did she really think there was a new life waiting for her at the other end of the plane trip? Was she that foolish? And she'd never been on her own in a big city in her life. She'd heard so many stories about San Francisco. . . .

Shelby clenched her fists around her burdens and marched toward the jetway. She wouldn't listen to the doubts. This was her chance. Maybe nothing would come of it, but she had to at least try. She'd felt a stirring in her heart for months, an unnamed dissatisfaction. She'd asked God about it but had gotten no answer. Or could this be His answer?

By the time the plane landed at the San Francisco airport and she'd rented a sporty red Chrysler convertible, Scarlet was whining to be let out. The dog licked her face excitedly when she opened the cage door. Shelby laughed and took her out. She hopped in the car and set Scarlet in the passenger seat. Putting the top down, she lifted her face to the California sunshine. All her fears and misgivings evaporated like the morning mist.

Shelby fastened her seat belt and put on her sunglasses. "Ready or not, here I come," she muttered.

❦

Jesse Titus surveyed the flotsam bobbing in the bay. A muscle in his jaw twitched, but he managed to keep his expression impassive. What was he going to do now?

Andy Everest, Jesse's best friend, leaned over and snagged a jagged board. He held it up, and Jesse saw the word ERING. It was all that was left of the boat's name, *Westering*. Andy's throat worked, and Jesse looked away. It was all he could do to control his own emotions; he couldn't bear to see the disappointment in his friend's face as well. Three years of training, gone like the tide.

"Do you have any idea what happened?" Andy whispered.

"The patrol says it was likely a gas leak and explosion," Jesse said. He couldn't keep the skepticism from his voice.

Andy seemed to ponder this announcement, and his face grew even whiter. "I don't believe it. I checked the auxiliary motor out myself just two days ago. It was in perfect order."

Jesse nodded. "I remember." He allowed a sigh to escape. "We'd never be able to prove sabotage."

"Maybe not, but we can't let Wilson get away with this!" Andy dropped the splintered board back into the water.

A wave caught it and pulled it beneath the pier. The rest of the remains of Jesse's pride and joy lay in scattered piles on the beach and in the water. Jesse felt as shattered as those boards. He took off his cap and raked a hand through his tight curls. His head felt swollen and fuzzy with lack of sleep.

"What are you going to tell the crew?"

Jesse put his cap back on and squinted into the sun. "I'm not giving up," he said. "We'll just have to charter a boat, that's all."

Andy gave a snort of disbelief. "Who would be fool enough to let us take a boat of theirs around Cape Horn? Especially without them captaining it?"

Jesse clenched his fists. He would find a way, somehow. "We have no choice," he said shortly. "The insurance won't pay up in time to buy a new boat. We *have* to find a substitute." He glanced at his friend when Andy made a sudden movement.

"I got it!" Andy said. "This race was all old man West's idea. His boats are just sitting in the harbor since he died. Surely his lawyer would let us take one of his, considering the circumstances."

"I don't know if there's one that is suitable," Jesse said thoughtfully.

"I know there is," Andy said, following Jesse to the pickup truck. He got in the passenger side and buckled his seat belt. "Remember *Jocelyn?*"

❧

The view from Watson Law Offices nearly took Shelby's breath away. The San Francisco Bay was a sapphire jewel in the sunshine. The Golden Gate Bridge was like a tiara over the city's crown jewel. Lew Watson cleared his throat as he entered the room, and Shelby turned from the magnificent view.

A thin man with round spectacles perched on the end of his nose and a nervous habit of chewing on his inner lip, Mr. Watson seated himself behind the gleaming mahogany desk and picked up a sheaf of papers. He cleared his throat again and peered through his glasses.

"It all seems quite in order, Ms. West. Your uncle was a thorough man. He left you an estate of five charter boats, his domicile at 122 Bay Drive, Sandy Cove, and the sum of five hundred thousand dollars."

Shelby caught her breath. Gripping the arms of the massive leather chair, she closed her eyes as her vision dimmed and swayed. Her blood pulsed in her ears.

"There is, however, one stipulation. ... ."

Shelby's heart dropped in a sickening swoop. She knew this was all too good to be true. Opening her eyes, she fastened her gaze on Mr. Watson's pompous face. His cheeks were much too plump for the rest of his body, she thought irrationally. "St–stipulation?" she stammered.

He steepled his fingers together. "I tried to talk him out

of it, but he prevailed." Watson's gaze dropped, and he cleared his throat again. "To inherit, you must take his favorite boat, the *Jocelyn*, on a trip around Cape Horn. You may have a crew, but the trip must be accomplished within six months of his death or the entire estate will be sold at auction, the proceeds going to the other recipients."

Shelby shook her head. Surely she didn't hear him right. "Excuse me?"

His brows drew together, and he pursed his lips. "You must sail the *Jocelyn* around Cape Horn by August 10 to inherit your uncle's property."

"B–but I don't know how to sail," Shelby said. "I don't even know how to swim."

Watson's frown deepened at her admission. "Then I would suggest you take lessons," he said. "As I understand, the trip around the Horn will take three to four months. That gives you nearly three months to learn."

Shelby rose shakily to her feet. "That's out of the question. I'm afraid I have to decline the offer." Her stomach plummeted sickeningly at the thought of being so far out on the ocean that she couldn't see land. It was out of the question.

"You're turning down your uncle's bequest?"

At any other time, Shelby would have smiled at the incredulity in the man's voice, but she was too upset to see much mirth in this situation. She slung her purse strap over her arm. "Thank you for your time, Mr. Watson." She should have known it was too good to be true. Five hundred thousand dollars! It was incomprehensible.

"Wait! You can stay in the house until the time is up."

She stopped and considered. "How long do I have?"

"Until August 10. You may turn in your expenses during

that time, and the estate will pay for them."

Shelby caught her breath. "You mean the estate will support me for six months? All my expenses?"

He nodded. "Right down to clothes and food. Everything. The estate will have to go through probate, so of course you won't be allowed to sell anything."

Her mind whirled. She could take six months off work and try to find a new life for herself. Was that a good thing or bad? She raised her gaze to meet Mr. Watson's anxious gray eyes. "I guess I could think about it," she said.

Relief lit his face. He opened his center drawer and pulled out a ring of keys. "Here are the keys to the house, the car, and your five boats." Stepping around the desk, he gave them to her then shook her hand. "Here are directions to the house and the boats. I wish you the best of luck."

"Do you have any idea why Uncle Lloyd left me this bequest? I barely knew him."

Mr. Watson shook his head. "I've no idea. Er, and I should mention, there are stipulations for the other recipient of your uncle's generosity as well." He frowned. "You should be glad you're not being asked to do what your uncle demands of *him*. If he should fail in his assignment, you will inherit another two hundred thousand dollars."

Shelby frowned. "I don't need anything more. I just want to find out why he left me this in the first place."

He tilted his head to one side and looked her over. "You have something of the look of your uncle about you. I will be very surprised if you ever give me back those keys," he said.

Shelby smiled. "I'm afraid I'm not nearly as brave as my uncle was."

He lifted the corners of his lips, but the smile didn't reach his eyes. "We'll see."

Her heart thumped uneasily as she let herself out of the office. If he knew how deep her fear of the water went, he wouldn't make such a sweeping prediction. She longed for adventure, but the kind she preferred was merely dipping her toes into the waves, then lying on a towel in the sunshine.

She walked through the parking lot and found her car. Scarlet yipped in joy when she opened the door and got in. She lowered the top again and headed out of the city.

Shelby located a contemporary Christian station, cranked up the radio, then tromped on the gas pedal. The sooner she blew the smog out of her lungs, the better.

Crowded traffic gave way to rolling green hills and meandering roads. Following the instructions the attorney had given her, she drove along the rocky coastline until she reached a road that dipped down toward the water.

A tiny fishing hamlet, seemingly right from the pages of a travel magazine, glimmered in the sunshine below her. "Oh, Scarlet, look!" The dog perked up her ears at the sound of her name and whined.

Shelby's spirits lifted at the sight of the sailboats dotting the dock, and the quaint seaside buildings and homes. And this would be home for six months. A smile curved her lips. She drove slowly past weathered store fronts and found Bay Drive. It wasn't much more than a rutted track that ran along the water. She turned onto it and scanned the houses for numbers. She jammed on the brakes. There it was.

The house was a stately Victorian with a widow's walk ringed by iron railing. From the moment she set her eyes on it, Shelby knew she could never let it be sold to the highest bidder. It was her dream home, right down to the stained glass over the bay window. She felt as though she'd come home. Her shoulders tight, her hands gripping the wheel, she stared at the house.

She'd seen this house in pictures, she realized—one of her aging great-grandparents sitting on the steps and another of her mother at the age of twelve, posed in front of the bougainvillea with her brother, Joe. Maybe that's why she felt such a strange sense of possessiveness.

Scarlet licked Shelby's chin and brought her back to her senses. "Sorry, Sweetie." She gave a sigh of pure contentment, then drove the car into the driveway and got out. She dropped Scarlet into the yard to stretch and dug out the keys from inside her purse. If the inside was as darling as the outside, she had to find a way to keep the house.

But could she leave her comfortable life back in Indiana? Her friends? Her church? All the familiar things of home tugged at her heart. Shelby gazed at the house again. It was perfect. And if she was ever going to break out of her rut, what better time than now?

The well-oiled lock opened on the first try. Shelby waited until her eyes adjusted to the gloom a bit then stepped inside with Scarlet on her heels. She caught her breath. The entry hall was lovely, with polished wood floors and ivory walls. Her steps echoed as she walked into the parlor. Obviously a man's home, this room was paneled with walnut. The overstuffed furniture invited her to sit in front of the fireplace and relax.

Half-dazed, she wandered through the house. A living room, dining room, library, and kitchen made up the downstairs, while upstairs she found four bedrooms and two baths. Though not matching her taste in decor, she knew what it could be with a little work. Her excitement grew at the thought of redoing the house and living here with the sound of the surf drifting in the open windows. And her mother's arthritis would probably improve in the warm weather.

The roar of the surf drew her to the window in the upstairs landing. Whitecaps were breaking on the shore. Shelby stared at the boats on the water. The only way to keep the house was to overcome her fear of the water. She didn't know if she could do it, but in that moment, she knew she had to try.

"Hello in the house." A man's voice echoed up the open staircase.

Shelby came to the top of the stairs and looked down to the open front door. The man standing at the door looked up, and when his gaze met hers, her stomach took a dizzying dive toward her feet.

Easily six-feet-six-inches tall, his shoulders filled the doorway and blocked out the sun. She'd have to look up to him, no question about that. He wore a shirt that said Titus Architects and denim shorts that showed his tanned, muscular legs. His black hair clung to his head in tight curls and framed a strong-jawed face that held a bit of humor in the eyes and firm lips. Not exactly handsome, but a dangerous man when it came to matters of the heart. Not that she was susceptible.

Shelby picked up Scarlet for protection and slowly descended the stairs, stopping in front of the man. "Can I help you?"

He frowned at the dog in her arms. "I should turn you in for canine abuse," he said. He reached over and pulled the bow from Scarlet's hair. The traitorous dog licked him and practically smiled at the attention.

This was her dog, and he was standing in her home. What right did he have to criticize? She frowned at him, but that didn't cause the wattage on his grin to go down at all. She snatched the bow from his hand. "Who are you, and what do you want?" Her voice sounded shrill and peevish in her ears, and she winced inwardly.

The man smiled. The flash of white teeth did something funny to her insides, and she steeled herself against his magnetism. He likely was married or had a girlfriend. And even if he didn't, he wouldn't be interested in her. Most men were put off by her size. She hadn't worn a size six since she was eight, though she'd managed to keep her generous curves restrained in a size fourteen for the past year. The massive bulk of this man made her feel petite for the first time in her life.

He pulled one tanned hand from his pocket and held it out. "Jesse Titus," he said. "I'm interested in chartering one of your boats."

Shelby shook his hand. She should tell him she wouldn't charter him a boat. What did she know about such matters? But maybe this was the Lord's answer to her dilemma about how to keep the house. If there was any chance of doing that, she had to learn to sail.

She stared at him thoughtfully then stepped away from the door. "Come in and let's talk," she said.

two

The woman was going to be trouble. Jesse stepped into the dim parlor and thrust his hands into his pockets. The tense undercurrent in the woman's tone set his teeth on edge. He'd given her his best smile, and she hadn't been fazed.

She was fiddling with the drapes, trying to open them, and he thought about helping her, but he had a feeling she wouldn't take kindly to the idea that she wasn't competent. Dressed in a severe gray suit with not a ruffle or bit of lace to soften the man-tailored blouse, her attire warned him that here was a woman who expected the world to take her seriously. He wondered about her profession. She looked like a lawyer or an executive of some kind.

The room smelled musty, as though it had been closed up awhile. Nice, though. A man's room, he thought in approval. No cow figurines or dried flower arrangements— none of that cutesy country decor his sister loved. That six-foot-long couch would be just perfect for watching football.

He glanced at his hostess again. She was quite a looker. Probably every bit of six feet tall with statuesque proportions that would make any man take a second look. She didn't slouch like so many tall women did. Gorgeous burnished hair that he wished he could see loosed from its restraining bun, and green eyes that tilted up at the corners. Her mouth was maybe a little wide for true beauty, but it looked as though it was meant for kissing. Not that he cared, of course. He was here for one thing, and one thing only.

The woman finally succeeded in opening the drapes and turned toward him. Sunshine arced off her hair in a blaze of red and gold. Tearing his eyes away, he cleared his throat. "I don't believe you mentioned your name." He offered her a smile and his hand.

She hesitated then shook his hand. "Shelby West." Gesturing toward the couch he'd been ogling, she sat in the overstuffed chair opposite the couch and folded her hands in her lap.

He gingerly lowered his bulk onto the couch and sat back. It was her move. She obviously had something on her mind.

"You said you wanted to charter one of my boats?"

Jesse leaned forward. "*Jocelyn*, actually."

"Why that boat in particular?" Her green eyes stared intently into his face.

He shifted a bit at her stare. Now came the tricky part. But she seemed to be a novice. Maybe she wouldn't realize how unorthodox his request was. "My boat was destroyed last night. I have to find a replacement until the insurance money pays up. The Southern Cup race around Cape Horn begins in three days. I've been training for years for this race." He leaned forward and gazed into her eyes.

Her eyes widened, and a strange expression crossed her face. Jesse thought it was a mixture of triumph and fear, but neither emotion made any sense to him.

"Cape Horn!" Her eyes widened even more, and a sudden flare of terror was replaced by a suppressed excitement.

"At least you've heard of the Cape and its dangers. Sailors call the Southern Ocean 'Dead Men's Road,' and the old-timers labeled their maps of that area *hic sunt dracones*— Here are dragons."

"I'd like to go with you," she said.

She wasn't as smart as she looked. "I've been training for this race for years," he said through gritted teeth. "You don't just walk aboard a boat and set sail for a place like Cape Horn. My crew is assembled, a good one I might add, and I've paid the fee, which nearly bankrupted me. I can't sit by and let a hundred thousand dollars fly out the window just because you take a fancy to accompany me. This is my one shot, my only shot at the Cup." He debated about telling her just why it was so important to him and decided she didn't need to know that. Not yet.

"I'll make it worth your while," she said. She laced her fingers together and bit her lip. "You may use *Jocelyn* at no cost."

"No cost?"

His rising elation dimmed. She was still a novice. A determined novice with a boat. "What kind of sailing experience have you had?" It might not be too bad if she was race certified. While sailing Cape Horn demanded experience, she wouldn't slow him down too badly with his experienced crew if she could at least pull her own weight on light duty.

"None." She rose and paced over to the fireplace, then reached up to straighten a picture.

"None, as in no race training?"

"None, as in I've never sailed."

Were her hands shaking? That made no sense to Jesse. If

she was frightened of sailing, why force him to take her along? But he'd get another boat before he agreed to her preposterous request.

Shelby turned back toward him and stared at him impassively. She'd make a good chess player, he decided. Not a muscle twitched in that pale skin.

"I'd prefer to keep it on a professional level and merely pay you for the use of the boat," he said at last. "If you're looking for sailing lessons, you should try something a little less grueling than the Southern Cup. Cape Horn is no place for a novice." He shook his head. "I couldn't take an inexperienced sailor into those waters."

She bit her lip and thrust her trembling hands into the pockets of her jacket. "Then I'm afraid we have nothing more to say to one another," she said. "I'll see you out."

"Now wait a minute," he began.

She held up a hand. "Those are my conditions, Mr. Titus. If you want my boat, you must take me as well."

He clamped on the anger building in his chest. He'd been right, she was trouble. He could tell by her manner that she was used to making decisions and having them carried out. Well, he was going to disabuse her of the notion that *he* had to jump at her beck and call. His lips tight, he brushed past her and stalked toward the door. He'd just have to find another boat.

"Mr. Titus," she called after him.

He stopped with his hand on the door.

"If you happen to change your mind, I'll be up late tonight unpacking."

"I won't change my mind," he snapped. Why had God made such illogical creatures as women? He slammed the door behind him and felt a stab of remorse at the sound. He was behaving like a child himself. So she wouldn't charter her boat to him; she had that right. He would just find one somewhere else.

But four hours later, he and Andy had to admit defeat. No one was willing to risk a boat to the Southern Ocean, not at any price.

"Well, I guess that's the end of the road for us." Andy's voice was morose, and he stared out to sea with a look of longing on his face. "Maybe next year." He turned and stared at Jesse. "Unless you change your mind about the *Jocelyn*."

"No!" He thought of the paper West's lawyer Watson had given him. Papers that still sat unopened on his overflowing desk. He wouldn't allow himself to be drawn into West's schemes and machinations. Andy would think him a fool if he knew he had turned down that kind of money. And now, here were other circumstances that were forcing him to reconsider. His father's phone call for one. It wouldn't matter if he was sure he would win the race, but with the Southern Cup, nothing was certain. Shelby would be his insurance, if he chose to take it.

"I could teach her the basics in the next couple of days." Andy's voice was tinged with desperation.

Jesse knew this was probably Andy's last chance to get away, too. He and his wife Heather planned to start a family next year. A family man couldn't afford to take six months off from work. Heather wanted to go as well, and she would certainly not leave an infant next year to go gallivanting to the bottom of the world. It was this year or not at all. And he couldn't afford to lose the race fee—his *family* couldn't afford to lose it.

Andy seemed to sense his hesitation. "The other girls will take her under their wing. She can stay below in the worst of the weather. We can do it, Jesse!"

Did he have the right to make a decision for all of them based on his pride? Jesse ground his teeth together. "All right, all right," he said, throwing his hands up in the air. "But she's *your* responsibility. I want to have as little to do with her as possible. She and I are like oil and water. We just don't mix."

❦

Shelby straightened and pressed a hand into the crook of her back. The bedroom was now clean and all of her belongings put away. She'd called her mother and told her about the house and the money. Her mother's pathetic eagerness to move to California with her had sealed her determination. She had to find a way to keep her inheritance and care for her mother. But right now, all she wanted was to crawl into bed and forget her dilemma for a few hours.

The bed was a half-canopy like she'd seen in magazines. The cream coverings on the bed and the canopy were hand crocheted, and she'd enjoyed poking into the drawers of the antique dresser. Everything was meticulously clean. Uncle Lloyd's cleaning woman had maintained the home even after his death.

Mom said the contents of this room had belonged to Shelby's great-grandmother. It gave her a strange connection to the past to think about snuggling under the quilt and sleeping in the same bed great-grandma Bessie had slept in.

The more she explored the house, the more she loved it. But with her fear of the water, it was madness to even consider trying to sail around the Horn with a mere three days' training. Those things Jesse had said about the Southern Ocean had brought the sharp taste of fear to her mouth. She should take lessons and make the voyage after she'd had some experience. She had six months to accomplish Uncle Lloyd's stipulations.

She had a feeling the trip itself held the key to why Uncle Lloyd had named her as his beneficiary. His action made no sense. There were others in the family with closer ties to him. Palmer Wilson or her own mother, for example. Why would he leave it to a great-niece? The lawyer didn't mention who the other recipient was. Maybe Palmer had inherited a sum, too. Did the Horn itself hold the key to the mystery? She had to find out, no matter how frightened she was. And she was terrified.

She went to the bathroom and turned on the tap in the oversized claw-foot tub. Pulling her hair back in a scrunchie, she washed her face and brushed her teeth. A chime from downstairs startled her. The doorbell? Who would come calling at this hour? It was after ten.

Turning off the water, she went down the hall and looked down the stairway at the entry door. Her heart thudded, and she castigated herself for being such a frightened ninny. Scarlet hid behind her leg and whimpered. A hulking shadow was visible through the window in the door. Shelby put a hand to her throat and swallowed hard. She wished she had a weapon. Scarlet whimpered again, and Shelby picked her up and started down the staircase.

Scarlet whimpered in her arms and buried her head in

her neck. "A fine guard dog you are," she whispered.

She stopped at the second step from the bottom. "Who—who's there?" she called.

"Jesse Titus."

She let out the breath she'd been holding and hurried to the door. Flipping on the entry light, she opened the door. "You scared the daylights out of me," she said.

"Sorry."

He didn't sound or look sorry as he strode past her into the entry. His brows were drawn together in a thunderous expression of displeasure as he crossed his arms over his chest and glowered at her.

Her heart sank. There was only one reason he would return—he must not have been able to find another boat. "Mr. Titus, I didn't expect to see you again." Though she had to find a way to go around the Horn, she didn't have to go with this man on a moment's notice. She must have been mad to make the offer.

His glower darkened. "I find I have no choice but to accept your offer, Miss West. As you surely knew when you made it." He uncrossed his arms and pointed a finger at her. "But don't think it's going to be easy. I expect you to pull your own weight aboard ship. We have three days to teach you the rudiments of sailing, and you'll be so tired by the time I'm done with you, you'll wish you had agreed to stay home."

Shelby's temper flared. She'd been on the verge of allowing him to lease the boat without taking her along, but his disdain was a goad to her pride. "I think not, Mr. Titus. I've never been afraid of hard work or learning something new. And you needn't blame me for your misfortune. You're the one who managed to wreck his boat three days before the big race."

He clenched his fists at his side, and a muscle in his jaw jumped. "You know nothing about that," he said shortly.

Her stab of victory at the way her shaft had gone home faded. "True," she admitted. "But you know nothing about me, either."

His jaw relaxed, and he nodded. "Tell me, Miss West, why would you want to go on such a dangerous trip when you obviously are frightened of the very idea of sailing?"

She thought she'd managed to cover her fear. Forcing a smile to her face, she shrugged. "If I'm going to own a charter business, I'm going to have to know something about it."

"But you don't have to round the Cape to know enough to take vacationers out on a pleasure trip." He crossed his arms over his chest again and stared at her with puzzled eyes.

"I have my reasons," she said. Turning away from his probing gaze, she stepped to the door and opened it. "My bath water is getting cold, and I'm tired," she said. "What time shall we meet in the morning?"

He stared at her for a moment longer before shrugging and moving toward the door. "I'll see you at the dock at six."

"Six!" The time change and jet lag had left her drooping with fatigue. She had planned to sleep in and putter around the house all day. She stiffened at the amusement in his face. She would show him. "Fine," she snapped. "Good night!"

She shut the door in his smirking face and waited until

she heard his footsteps move away before turning off the porch light and hurrying back upstairs. What had she gotten herself into?

The next morning, Shelby groaned when the alarm went off. Rolling over, she hit the snooze button and lay in the dark with her eyes open. In truth, she'd been awake for at least an hour. Her internal body clock was still set to Indiana time and thought it was eight o'clock. She dreaded the day ahead. The thought of admitting that she didn't even know how to swim made her stomach tighten. She could only imagine what the supercilious Jesse Titus would make of that.

The alarm gave its shrill warning again, and she sat up. Shutting it off, she forced herself out of bed and padded to the closet. She quickly dressed in sharply pressed slacks, with a blouse and jacket. Power dressing might help her face the day ahead. Shoving her feet into her size eleven shoes, she twisted her hair on top of her head and marched downstairs before she lost her nerve.

Scarlet followed her to the kitchen. Wagging her tail, she nosed her food dish plaintively. "All right, all right," Shelby muttered. She opened a can of dog food, ladled it into the dog's dish, then munched an apple for breakfast while she read her Bible. Looking up a couple of verses on fear, she committed the best one to memory.

While she and Scarlet went for a run along the beach, she recited the verse under her breath. "For God did not give us a spirit of timidity, but a spirit of power, of love and of self-discipline." By the time she and Scarlet stepped onto the dock, she felt fortified. She might be afraid, but she was determined Jesse Titus wouldn't know it.

Dawn glimmered on the horizon, but the black water still looked menacing. Shelby wondered what kind of terrors lurked beneath the waves. Sharks? Giant squids? Suppressing a shudder, she squared her shoulders and walked down the dock.

A broad-shouldered figure loomed out of the shadows, and she caught her breath. Jesse's deep voice vibrated along her nerves.

"There you are. I was beginning to wonder if you'd chickened out." He came toward her, and the lights along the dock illuminated his face with its planes and angles. Frowning, he stared at her feet. "You brought that fluffy excuse for a dog along?"

Shelby scooped Scarlet up. "I couldn't leave her alone in a strange place all day."

"What a darling dog!" Another figure stepped out of the shadows. The woman reached out a hand to Scarlet, and the dog wriggled with delight.

In her midtwenties, the woman was petite, about five-two, with blond ringlets clustered around a pixy face. Her big blue eyes were round with delight. "Can I hold him?"

"Her," Shelby corrected. She handed Scarlet to the woman. Was she with Jesse? The dismay she felt at the thought discomfited her. The man could date whomever he wanted, and it certainly wouldn't be her.

Jesse sighed. "Miss West, this is Heather Everest, one of the crew. Her husband Andy is first mate. Heather, this is the *Jocelyn's* owner, Shelby West."

Relief flooded her. The cute blond was already married and was no competition. Not that she was competing, either, she told herself. She covered her sense of inadequacy in the face of such a feminine creature with a warm smile.

Heather gave Scarlet one last pat and put her down. "I've heard a lot about you, Miss West," she said, extending her hand.

"I'll bet," Shelby said with a sideways glance at Jesse. "Please call me Shelby, both of you."

Heather's eyes crinkled adorably as she smiled. "Don't let Jesse's gruffness fool you," she said. "He's really a lamb, not a lion."

The "lamb" glowered at Heather, and she laughed and poked him in the stomach. Shelby gulped when his frown turned to a grin, and he laughed. His grin still lingered when he turned his attention to her, and the leftover warmth in his eyes made her mouth go dry. The man was way too attractive for her peace of mind.

Jesse's smile faded. "You'd better keep that dog below deck," he said. "If she goes overboard, a fish will have her for breakfast."

Shelby gulped. "I'll watch her. She'll get used to the boat. I can't leave her behind when we sail; there's no one to care for her."

"There are kennels," Jesse said. "I can recommend a good one."

Heather poked him again. "Jesse, you heartless thug! I wouldn't leave such an adorable puppy in a kennel, either. I'll help Shelby look out for Scarlet. You'll never know she's aboard."

Jesse sighed. "I know when I'm out-gunned," he said grudgingly. "Where are the rest of the crew?"

Heather chuckled. "They're already aboard *Jocelyn*, checking out the equipment."

"We might as well join them." He stood back and motioned for Shelby and Heather to pass. Heather led the way, and Shelby's heart plummeted as she moved toward the dinghy that would take them to the boat. The tiny boat bobbed in the waves, and Shelby clenched her hands into fists. Jesse's keen dark eyes probed her face, and she imagined he could see her terror.

Taking several deep breaths, she muttered under her breath. "God did not give us a spirit of timidity, but a spirit of power, of love and of self-discipline."

"What did you say?" Jesse tilted his head to one side and stared at her.

"Nothing," she said hastily. "I was talking to myself."

He nodded as though to say it was nothing more than he expected of her. He handed her a life jacket, and she put it on. Heather hopped into the boat and turned with an outstretched hand to help Shelby. Panic rose in Shelby's chest, and she felt as though she might choke from the terror that squeezed the air from her lungs. Spots swam in her vision, and she froze at the pier.

Then Jesse's warm fingers grasped her arm, and his deep voice was in her ear. "It's all right," he whispered. "You're going to be fine. Take a deep breath. I've got you. Put one foot down into the boat; I won't let you fall."

Dimly, she clung to his muscular arm and eased one foot down into the boat. Heather took her other hand, and Jesse propelled Shelby down into the boat gently. The boat rocked sickeningly, and Shelby feared she would compound her disgrace by throwing up. Then it steadied, and she found herself sitting on the seat. Jesse scooped up Scarlet and stepped into the boat himself.

Shelby caught her breath and squeezed her eyes shut as the boat rocked again, then Jesse dropped the dog into her lap, and she clutched Scarlet as though clinging to a lifeline. Cautiously opening her eyes, she found Heather staring at her with sympathy in her blue eyes. The boat began to move, and Shelby's gaze flew to Jesse. He sat gazing out to sea with a rapt look on his face, as though he was heading home to a beloved wife. She felt a twinge of envy. Was there a woman in his life whom he looked at like that?

Waves slammed against the boat, and Shelby wanted to shout for him to take her back, but all that issued from her lips was a faint whisper that only Scarlet heard. The little dog whimpered with her and licked her chin as Shelby watched the receding pier grow farther away. She would never survive this trip.

three

Jesse maneuvered the dinghy beside the *Jocelyn* and tied it fast. The dinghy rocked when he stood, and Shelby's face whitened. She puzzled him. Why did she push herself so much by coming on this trip? Most people who were that terrified of the water resisted all efforts to overcome their fear. She was a brave woman.

He held out his hand. "Let's get aboard."

Her green eyes grew round, and her lips trembled, but she took a deep breath and slowly stood. Heather got to her feet and scurried up the ladder. Shelby watched her through narrowed eyes, then squared her shoulders.

Jesse held out his hand. "You'd better give me the mongrel. You'll need both hands for the ladder." Scarlet licked his chin when he took her, and he stifled a grin. Much as he normally disliked dogs, she was an engaging little ball of fluff. He tucked her inside his jacket and zipped it up so that only her head poked through.

Shelby stepped gingerly over to the ladder and stared up toward the deck. "What if I fall into the water? I can't swim."

"You can't even swim?" Jesse saw the way she flinched at his harsh tone and softened his voice. "You have a life jacket on. You won't drown." He itched to know just what drove her to come out here like this. But she disliked him, so he wasn't likely to find out.

Shelby nodded, then put her hands on the ladder. Her

33

knuckles white, she pressed her face against the rungs.

Jesse put his hands on her waist. "One step at a time. Don't look down, just focus on the ladder. I won't let you fall." Her hair smelled fresh and clean, like spring rain. He had to resist the impulse to pluck the pins holding it in place and let it fall to her shoulders.

Shelby nodded, then put her left foot on the first rung. He could feel her trembling, and his respect increased yet another notch. Courage wasn't the absence of fear, it was the strength to act in the presence of that fear, and Miss Shelby West possessed more raw courage than he'd ever seen. He lifted her slightly, and she began to climb. Heather peered over the top and called encouragement down to her.

In moments, Shelby was at the top of the ladder, and Heather was helping her onto the deck. Jesse breathed a sigh of relief. He paid the skipper and clambered up the ladder himself. Heather was showing her around the deck. Shelby appeared calm and in control again, and if he didn't know better, Jesse would have thought he imagined the way her body had trembled.

Growing up in a family of four boys, women were enigmas to Jesse, and this particular one even more so. What could be so all-fired important about learning to sail that she drove herself this way when she was so terrified? She intrigued him with her generous mouth and smoky green eyes that held a hint of uncertainty. But he'd never understand women.

Those eyes were wide with apprehension now. He smiled reassuringly and handed her the dog. "Ready to take a tour and have your first lesson in sailing?"

Before she could answer, a voice hailed them from the

port side. "Ahoy, *Jocelyn!*"

A speedboat ripped through the water toward them. The skipper cut the motor, and it pushed its wake toward them as it slowed and then stopped. The man pushed back his white cap and smiled. About thirty-five, he was of average height but muscular, with blond hair and pale gray eyes.

"I'm looking for Shelby West," the man called. "I was told she was aboard."

Shelby's eyebrow's arched, and she came to the railing. "I'm Shelby," she said.

"I'm Palmer Wilson." His eyes crinkled at the corners when he smiled. "I think we're sort of related. Your great-uncle Lloyd was my stepfather for a time."

Shelby exhaled, and the corners of her mouth lifted. "Palmer! I've heard a lot about you." She leaned over the railing, then seemed to remember the water below her. "Would you like to come aboard?"

Jesse kept a rein on his emotions. His inclination was to toss Palmer into the drink and hold him there until he confessed to sinking the *Westering*. He reminded himself of what the Bible said about forgiveness, but seeing Palmer standing there with that smug, knowing grin on his face was still hard to take. And they were wasting time with chitchat. It would take every minute of daylight for the next three days to stuff as much knowledge into Shelby's head as possible before they sailed. But it was her boat. He compressed his lips and stepped away from the ladder so Palmer could come aboard.

Palmer was dressed in white shorts and shirt with navy trim. He looked like a natty playboy who was masquerading as a sailor. Jesse barely managed to keep his lips from curling in contempt. The man fooled most people, at least at first, but raging ambition dwelt beneath that smiling exterior, ambition that let nothing stand in its way.

Shelby seemed impressed, though. Her wide mouth was stretched in a welcoming smile, and her green eyes sparkled. "I had planned to see if you were in town," she said. "I'd love to talk with you and find out more about Uncle Lloyd."

Jesse clamped his teeth together. It was none of his business.

"Shall we dine together tomorrow night?" Palmer took her hand and raised it to his lip.

Jesse shot a look of incredulity to Heather, and she rolled her eyes.

Shelby stared at Jesse uncertainly. "I—I'm not sure when we'll get back to shore at night," she began.

Jesse cut in. "Not until after dark." He raised his eyebrows and jerked his head toward the sun. "We're wasting today's daylight as it is," he said meaningfully.

A tide of heightened color suffused Shelby's pale, lightly freckled skin. "Of course," she said. She pulled her hand away from Palmer. "Shall we say eight? That should give me time to shower and change."

Palmer's gaze lingered on her pink cheeks. "I shall look forward to it," he said softly. He saluted, then scrambled down the ladder to his speedboat.

"Oh, brother!" Jesse shook his head as the boat engine roared to life and carried Palmer away. "He thinks he's God's gift to women."

Shelby flushed again. "I'm not looking for a man."

No, she was just looking to ruin Jesse's plans of winning the Southern Cup and a prize of two hundred thousand dollars to boot. "Can we get down to business?" he asked brusquely.

Her eyes flashed at his peremptory tone, but she inclined her head. "I can see you're going to be a slave driver."

"You've got *that* right," Heather muttered under her breath.

Jesse frowned. Now she had his own crew questioning his orders. It would be a miracle if they even placed in the finals of the race. "I know Andy is in town buying supplies, but where are the rest of the crew?"

Heather shrugged. "Nick and Brian are below deck checking out the food and supplies that are already onboard, and Twila is putting her gear away."

"I had hoped to be underway by now," Jesse said.

"I'll show our guest around," a throaty voice said.

They all turned as Twila Connors came toward them. A slender woman with smooth black skin and dark eyes, Twila held out a welcoming hand to Shelby.

"Twila is the resident mother aboard ship," Jesse said with a grin. "You're what, Twila, maybe forty? Not old enough to be our mother, but she sure gives good advice. Feel free to wake her up for a midnight talk anytime." His gaze lingered on her face. "You look a little pale today. Seasick from being a landlubber too long?" He grinned.

Twila laughed, then spoke in a soft Haitian accent. "I was born at sea, and you know it, Jesse." She turned to Shelby. "But Jesse's right about one thing, Child. It's good to have you aboard, and you can come to me when this big lug gets too bossy."

Shelby's face brightened at the kind words. "I might have to do that," she said shakily.

"Twila, would you want to show Shelby a few things? She might take them better coming from you." Jesse couldn't resist the stab at their guest.

Twila wagged a red-tipped finger at him. "You throwin' your weight around with this child already, Jesse? Come with me, Shelby. You don't have to put up with any guff from Jesse. He's a lamb, really."

"So I've been told," Shelby said.

The way she lifted one eyebrow told Jesse she didn't believe that statement for one minute. And he was determined to keep it that way.

❦

Shelby's fear began to abate in Twila's calming presence. The ache in her jaw from clenching her teeth eased, but she clung to the railing as Twila showed her around.

"You know your directions aboard ship?" she asked.

Shelby shook her head. The rest of them must think she was a total imbecile to come aboard without a clue in the world about sailing.

"The front end of the boat is called the bow, the back end is aft or stern. The right is starboard and the left is port. You have to learn that first," Twila said. She strolled along the starboard side and pointed to the sail. "The setup of sails and spars is called the rig or rigging."

Twila's voice droned on, but Shelby was barely aware of it. A rumble under her feet told her Jesse had started the engines. Andy must have arrived, and they would soon be moving out to sea. Her mouth went dry. She clutched the railing with a white-knuckled grip. Resting her chin on Scarlet's fluffy head and inhaling her familiar doggy scent, she managed a smile and followed Twila to the doghouse leading to the living quarters below deck.

In the salon below, the strum of the engine was louder, but at least she couldn't see the ocean waves from here. Twila introduced her to Brian Daniels, an intense man of thirty with brooding dark eyes; he smiled and held her hand a bit too long when they exchanged greetings.

Shelby felt a sense of vertigo as the boat pulled away from her moorings. She cast a panicked stare toward Twila, and the older woman pressed her hand reassuringly.

"Let's go topside," Twila said. "It's easier to adjust to the movement when you can see the water."

Shelby doubted that, but she followed her new friend up the ladder to the deck. The wind caught her hair and tugged strands loose, then whipped it into her mouth.

Twila saw her plight and ducked down below again. She reappeared a few minutes later with a hat. "Here, stuff your hair up in this."

Shelby gave her a grateful smile and corralled her hair into the green hat. The wind touched the back of her neck, and she shivered. What was she doing here? She must be mad. Her glance was drawn to Jesse. He stood at the helm of the boat, his muscular legs planted in that wide sailor stance, his eyes scanning the horizon.

He saw her perusal and motioned to her. "Come here and meet Andy," he shouted over the sound of the wind and the engines.

Still gripping the railing, she made her way to his side. A short, stocky man of about thirty, Andy had an open, engaging grin and light blue eyes. A short, neatly trimmed beard did nothing to hide his good nature.

He took her hand in a firm grip. "So you're the woman

who saved our bacon." His smile widened.

"I don't know about that. . . ," Shelby began.

"Believe me, we were up a creek without a paddle." He shot a look at Jesse. "He might not show it, but we're all very grateful. All our training would have been for nothing."

Jesse's jaw tightened, and Shelby sensed Andy's effusive thanks had irritated him. He probably was still mad that she hadn't let him take the boat without her. And she still might let him. She was not enjoying this sailing experience, and they were still in calm waters. Already her stomach was beginning a slow roll that left her feeling vaguely uneasy. Not nauseous yet, but its promise was hovering nearby like the schools of silvery fish that followed the boat.

She should take more time becoming accustomed to the water and go with a skipper who didn't make her feel incompetent. Shelby was used to being in control, and this feeling of inadequacy was unpleasant.

If the image of her mother's fingers gnarled with arthritis hadn't swept over her at that moment, she would have told Jesse to take her to shore, and then she would have headed to the airport. Her mother deserved to live in a mild climate in comfort. And Shelby was the only one who could make that dream come true. She squared her shoulders; she could do this. She *had* to do this.

Jesse stopped the engines. "Time for your first lesson," he said. "The first thing you always have to be aware of is the wind. Where is it? In your face, from the side, or behind you. That determines what you do with the sail." He pointed to ribbons streaming from the sails. "Those are telltales. And at the top of the mast is the masthead fly. It points into the wind. We also have electronic indicators, but it's wise to learn to sail the old-fashioned way in case the electronics fail."

He then proceeded to speak incomprehensible terms that left Shelby's mind reeling. Words like "beam-reaching" and "close-hauled" and "tack." She tried not to let her bewilderment show, but he stopped in the middle of explaining degrees of wind.

"Enough of that. You'll figure it out soon enough." He motioned to Twila. "Why don't you show Shelby how to make some knots. That's one of the things we'll expect her to do anyway."

Knots? As in rope? A surge of encouragement lifted Shelby's spirits. She'd done well in Girl Scouts in the knot-tying area. Maybe this was something she could do.

Twila led her to the rigging and showed her the knots. It didn't look too difficult. She practiced tying overhand and underhand loops and brushed up on her square knots. Twila nodded in approval, and Shelby breathed a sigh of relief. At least she wasn't totally inept.

Even Jesse grunted in approval at the knots. "We'll make a sailor of you yet." He smiled and put a hand on her shoulder.

Shelby moved away from the warmth of his hand. It was too little, too late. He'd made no effort to hide his disapproval up to now, and she didn't trust him. He could just keep his distance, and she would keep hers. Though it was possible they might be friends by the time this voyage was over, she doubted it. Jesse Titus was a man who could hurt her, and she intended to keep up her guard around him.

The day sped by, and Shelby was drooping with fatigue when they headed back to their mooring. She tucked

Scarlet into her jacket and lined up at the ladder with the rest of the crew. When the time came for her to climb down the ladder to the waiting dinghy below, Shelby forced herself not to look at the water. She gripped the ladder rails and swung a foot out into space. Closing her eyes against the vertigo, her foot found the rung, and she eased her body over the side. One foot then the other. Hugging the side of the boat, she reached the dinghy, then Jesse's broad hands were at her waist.

He helped her into the boat. "Well done," he whispered.

She shot a glance at him to see if he was mocking her, but his dark eyes were full of approval. "Thanks," she said curtly. She sat on the seat, and the boat sped back toward the dock. Jesse helped her and the other women onto the pier, then waited until the men disembarked, also.

"Same time tomorrow," he said. His hand lingered on her arm again.

"I haven't decided yet," Shelby said.

His eyebrows shot up. "You haven't decided what?"

"Whether I'm going," she said. "Maybe you're right. This kind of trip is really beyond my ability."

He regarded her quietly with those enigmatic eyes. What was he thinking? He should be relieved she was considering staying behind, but Shelby saw no evidence of that in his steady gaze.

"I thought you had more spirit than that," he said quietly.

Was that really disappointment in his eyes? "And I thought that's what you wanted," she retorted.

"You did better than I was expecting."

"You can't back out now," Andy put in. "We have everything ready." Heather nodded in agreement.

"I would still let you take the boat," Shelby said. "I didn't mean I would back out of that."

"Child, we need you," Twila said. "We are one crew member short since Robert joined another team. It's too late to find someone else. You can't let us down."

They needed her? Shelby eyed Twila's smooth face suspiciously. She looked sincere, but Shelby found it hard to believe she would really be able to contribute any needed skill.

Twila smiled. "You did well today, Child. By the time we sail, you'll be an integral part of the team. You want to learn, and that's the first battle. Don't desert us now."

Shelby swallowed. After the stress of the day, she felt strangely weepy. "All right," she said.

Jesse fell into step beside her as they walked toward the boathouse. "How about dinner tonight?"

When she brought her startled gaze up to meet his, he smiled. "I thought we could discuss the trip, and I could give you some pointers on what to expect," he said.

Was that his real reason? She studied his hooded gaze, then nodded. "All right."

"I'll give you an hour to get ready," he said.

She watched him walk away with a shiver of apprehension. The thought of backing out had sustained her all day. Now she was back to facing the ocean with no sign of land. And that included her feelings for Jesse Titus.

four

The scent of apple-scented bubble bath still hung in the steamy bathroom. Luxuriating in the bubbles was Shelby's one concession to her femininity, and that was only because no one knew. She wiped the film from the mirror and stared into her own green eyes. They were shadowed with apprehension. All she really wanted to do was go to bed and pull the covers over her head. Instead, she had to smile and make polite conversation with a man she didn't know. Attractive though he was. But if he thought a date was going to get past her distrust of him, he had another think coming.

She took the blow-dryer and began to dry her hair. Tomorrow she would have dinner with another attractive man. She smiled and shook her head. Her mother would be proud. And what was behind the animosity she sensed between Palmer and Jesse? It had been as thick as the heavy fog in the bay. She pulled the top of her tousled mane of hair back in a french roll and applied a light touch of makeup. There was no reason not to try to look her best.

Selecting a green silk pantsuit, she quickly dressed and slipped her feet into flats. Satisfied with the image of the professional woman who looked back at her, she hurried downstairs, fed Scarlet, lit two scented candles, and turned on all the lamps in the living room. As if on cue, the doorbell rang. Straightening her shoulders, she went to the door.

Jesse's smile widened as his gaze lingered on her face.

"I like that color on you" was all he said, though his appreciative stare said more than his words. He stepped inside the hall and closed the door behind him.

Shelby wasn't used to fielding compliments. The heat of a blush warmed her cheeks, and she killed the smile hovering on her lips before it was born. "Thanks," she said. "Where are we going?" she asked, quickly changing the subject.

"I thought you might enjoy mingling with the natives tonight. The yacht club has a wonderful restaurant right on the water, and I've reserved a window seat where you can hear the waves." Jesse opened the door and gestured for her to exit ahead of him.

Shelby picked up her bag from the table and led the way to the car parked in the driveway. "Lovely car," she said. It was a Chrysler convertible—not new, but well maintained.

She snapped her seat belt and put her purse in her lap. Jesse slid into the car beside her and flashed her a wry grin. "One of these days I'll get a new one."

"Why? New isn't always better."

He smiled at her obvious admiration for the car. "Well, let me take it through its paces for you." He shoved it into gear, and as they hit the village limits, the car rocketed down the road.

Shelby caught her breath, and her grin widened. She loved speed. "Faster!" she shouted.

Jesse laughed, and the car responded to his urging. The turns above the water raced by them, and Shelby laughed with exhilaration. How could she feel such joy with the wind rushing through her hair, yet such terror when on the water? It was a puzzle to her. But at least here she could maintain the illusion of being a strong, competent woman.

Jesse downshifted, then pulled into the parking lot of a large building jutting over the water. She was still laughing, elated over the fun drive. She was free of her boring lifestyle, free of the old Shelby. All that was left to overcome was her fear of the water.

Painted in blue and white, the sign read FANTAIL RESTAURANT. Shelby waited for him to open the car door then slid out. The mingled aromas of seafood and steak were mixed with the sweet scent of fruit pies and grilling vegetables. Her mouth watered; she was ravenous.

Jesse held out his arm, and she laid her hand on it. It was hard with muscle, and heat scorched her cheeks. She didn't usually notice such things, and it mortified her that she was so aware of this man.

The restaurant atmosphere was dark and intimate. The maitre d' led them down a hall of dark wood, gleaming in the chandelier light overhead. Dressed in a tux, he wore a matching expression of supercilious reserve.

The maitre d' told them it would be few minutes before their table was ready. Jesse touched Shelby's hand. "I'll get us a drink. Pepsi okay?"

"Actually, I'd prefer water with lemon," she told him.

Jesse nodded. "I'll be right back." He walked to the drink area. A young woman of about Shelby's age stopped him as he turned with the glasses in his hand. Her long, dark hair fell in lustrous waves nearly to her waist, and she spoke with animation into his face. He bent his head to listen to her.

Talons of jealousy sank into Shelby's heart. The ferocity of her emotion surprised her. She didn't even know or trust the man; why on earth would she be jealous? Maybe it was the rude interruption of her prom-queen evening. She scowled. A man walking past quickened his gait at her fierce glare, and she hastily composed her countenance into a disinterested smile.

Jesse walked back to her. "Our table is ready."

He gave no hint of the woman's identity, and Shelby wasn't about to ask him. His big hand on her elbow guided her toward a table in the corner. Lights shone out over the water, and the sound of the surf echoed through the large windows. Shelby shivered at the sound.

The table was covered in a damask tablecloth with a fresh-flower centerpiece. Shelby slid into the seat farthest from the sound of the sea. The waitress handed them menus, and Shelby smiled her thanks and opened the menu. "What's good here? I'm famished. Sailing is harder work than I'd realized."

Jesse smiled. "You looked good on the deck, like you'd been born there. You'll find sailing is in your blood." He put his menu down. "I'm going to have the grilled salmon. It has a sugary kind of hickory glaze and is pretty good."

"Sounds yummy. That's what I'll have, too." Shelby closed her menu and laid it on the table.

The waitress took their order and soon returned with their salads. Shelby toyed with a piece of lettuce. She wasn't sure what to say to Jesse. He was too attractive to ignore. They'd best stick to business.

"So, just what will this voyage be like?" She kept her tone and expression light and interested.

Jesse was silent for a moment. "Exhausting, exhilarating, terrifying, and tremendous. One minute you'll be wondering whatever possessed you to attempt it, and the next you'll be ready to shout with exultation and sheer joy."

Her heart jumped, and a rapid pulse beat in her throat. She felt both repelled and attracted.

"When the trip is over, you'll have a sense of accomplishment and pride. But that won't be easy to come by when we're in the middle of the ocean for several months with no land in sight."

Her throat closed, and panic squeezed her chest. "No land for months?" she stammered.

He shook his head. "Just miles of endless ocean. We'll battle storms and becalmed winds, boredom and danger. Once we're on the ocean, there's no turning back."

She might as well give up now—she could never handle a journey like this. Despair gripped her. Why had she ever thought she could do this?

His dark eyes lit with amusement, and Shelby had the feeling he could read her mind. "Scared?"

For some reason, his taunt stiffened her spine and reminded her of just why she'd come. But her mother's needs and Shelby's feelings of restlessness were too private to discuss with a stranger. And for her own peace of mind, she needed to keep him at arm's length—stick to business.

She shrugged. "I want to conquer my fear. A Christian shouldn't go through life fearful when we have God's strength available to us."

His chocolate eyes widened. "A courageous statement."

Shelby laughed, noting his wry grin. "You can say that after seeing me quivering with fear today aboard the *Jocelyn?* You don't know how close I came to quitting. I still might."

"But you didn't. That says it all." He smiled, and the

curiously tense moment between them dissipated. "I'm starved. We'd better get some good eats in while we can—ship food leaves much to be desired. We take turns cooking, and no one enjoys it much. You wouldn't believe the types of things that can be freeze dried."

Shelby's spirits rose. "I can do that! I love to cook. In fact. . ." Her voice trailed off. Her dreams were too fragile to share with his skepticism.

"You're serious?" Jesse's voice rose above the lull in the orchestra, and several people looked their way. He grinned and lowered his voice. "The crew would rise up and call you blessed."

Shelby warmed at his stare of admiration. "I've never taken any special training, but I love to concoct new recipes. Could I pick out my own supplies?"

"We'll stop at the store on the way home tonight if you like. Tomorrow I'll show you the galley, and we'll see if you change your mind."

"Maybe I should ask the crew what kinds of meals they like before we buy the supplies."

"Surprise us. They can't be too picky—they've eaten my cooking." Jesse's grin widened. "This should be a new experience for you. We pack a lot of frozen and canned food. We'll stop at three ports during the trip to take on more supplies, but fresh foodstuffs won't last long."

"I love a challenge." Shelby's words were more confident than she felt. Now that the time had come to test herself, she couldn't still the flutter of apprehension that the thought of failure brought. When she got home, she would go through her favorite recipes and make up a shopping list. She prided herself on what she could do with canned food, and she'd get a chance to prove it. It was almost enough to still the fear that shouted for attention in her heart.

"Mind if I say grace?" Jesse asked.

Shelby smiled. "You're a believer?"

"For about five years. In fact. . ." He broke off and bowed his head.

What had he been about to reveal? Shelby bowed her head, but her thoughts whirled with questions. "In fact?"

He grinned. "Your uncle had something to do with that. We met right here about six years ago and got to talking. He invited me to go sailing with him the next day, and I saw something in his life that I'd been missing. Over the next year he witnessed to me, and God finally got through my hard head. I'll always be grateful to your uncle for that."

Shelby fell silent. There was more to Jesse Titus than a handsome exterior, and that made him even more danger- ous to her peace of mind.

They seemed to find a middle ground as they ate their dinner and chatted. Jesse glanced out over the water. "It's still light out. Want to stroll along the beach?"

Shelby hesitated. The thought of strolling along a beach at sunset with a man as attractive as Jesse made her mouth go dry. The sensation wasn't entirely appealing. She had a feeling Jesse might be dangerous to her heart. But her stomach did a little flip at the thought he might find her attractive. Or was it her boat he was attracted to?

She swallowed. "Why are you doing this?"

"Doing what?"

She gestured at the table. "This. This meal, the invitation

to walk the beach. You've hardly mentioned the trip, but you used that as an excuse for the invitation."

He raised an eyebrow. "Are you married or engaged?"

Heat scorched her cheeks. "You aren't attracted to me."

He smiled. "You think I have an ulterior motive for wanting to spend time with you? Any man in his right mind would be attracted to you."

"Men haven't exactly been beating my door down," she said dryly.

"Midwest men must be blind."

There was a note that rang true in his voice, and her discomfort increased. She knew better than to take his words at face value. He could have his pick of women; why would he be interested in her? She didn't possess an ounce of the soft fluffiness and flattering admiration that most men found attractive.

She chose not to answer his remark. "Since you haven't brought up the subject, I must. You know I'm not up to this trip, Jesse. You have to see that."

Jesse was silent a moment. "Ever seen a tide pool?" He rose and dropped a tip on the table.

"Tide pool?" What did that have to do with what she had just told him?

"If we hurry, we can get there while it's still low tide. I want to show you something."

She rose in bewilderment, and he guided her through the restaurant. Jesse opened the door for her and escorted her to the car. Within minutes they were speeding along the road. With the wind in her face and the roar of the engine filling her ears, she let her apprehension blow away like sand. His motives would surface sooner or later. In the meantime, there was nothing wrong with enjoying herself—so long as she protected her heart.

Jesse stopped the car at the top of a rocky cliff. "Come on, it's almost dark."

She flung open her car door and followed him. They picked their way down the rocks, Jesse stopping to assist her at treacherous areas. The scent of the sea filled her nostrils, and the crash of the waves against the rocks filled her with trepidation.

She slid her hands across the slick, algae-covered rocks as her fingers searched for purchase. If she should fall, the sea would carry her away. But Jesse's strong hand steadied her, and she clung to him as though to a lifeline.

He stopped at a flat ledge. "This is my favorite spot."

"This is a tide pool?" It didn't look like anything special to her. Just shallow water over bedrock.

Jesse squatted. "This is the low-tide area. Most of these animals at this level live their whole lives in this tiny pool." He pointed. "See the starfish clinging to the rocks? The rocks look kind of like lava rocks, don't they? The animals live in the holes in them. Look at the red Irish moss just under the mussels. It used to be collected along the coast of Maine and was used to thicken puddings, ice cream, and toothpaste."

Shelby squinted at the marine animals he pointed out. He knelt and coaxed a starfish loose from its moorings. Its legs draped around his hand. "The ocean is full of amazing and wonderful things." He put the starfish back into the water, and it slowly sank to the bottom of the pool.

"You think that makes this better? Those strange and wonderful creatures frighten me. Who knows what monsters lurk under those waves?" Shelby smiled, but her heart raced at the closeness of the black water.

Jesse stood. He smiled a curiously gentle smile that reached her heart. "You're like that starfish, Shelby. You've lived your life in the small tide pool, constrained by your fear. It's time to let the tide take you out into the wide world."

Her throat closed at his words. He was a strange man, barking orders one minute and saying something so poetic the next. She didn't know what to make of him. "I would think you would jump at the chance to be rid of me."

He shrugged. "We really do need you, Shelby. I know you don't believe it, but we do. Your courage is rather inspiring."

That word again—*courage*. She possessed very little of that. "Foolhardiness, you mean." He took her hand, and she caught her breath. She pulled her hand back and stepped away. "It's getting dark."

"You won't quit."

The commanding tone of his voice dared her to tell him she was afraid. The sound of the surf filled her ears, and the incoming tide foamed into the tide pool and hid the starfish from her gaze. Darkness crowded in and muffled his features with a safe anonymity. Shelby felt that she could tell him anything in that moment, even to revealing the secrets of her heart, the dreams that had brought her here. But a horn blared on the road above them, and the moment was lost.

Jesse's teeth gleamed in the darkness. "I'd better get you home before some of those creatures you're so afraid of come crawling up on shore." In spite of the amusement in his voice, he sounded as reluctant as she felt. He had her go before him, and several times his hands spanned her waist as he helped her climb back to the road.

They were both silent as they drove back to her house. She shivered, but not only from the cool night air. She was no closer to understanding this man, no closer to discovering why he wanted her to go along when he was so opposed to it just yesterday. It wasn't that he was suddenly smitten with an overwhelming attraction to her, of that she was certain.

He walked her to the door. His bulk loomed over her, and the musky scent of his cologne drew her, but she resisted the urge to step into his arms. What was wrong with her? She wasn't some petite little ball of fluff like Scarlet, who threw herself at every attractive man. She'd learned long ago that what was cute with a five-foot-two woman was ludicrous when she did it. Men didn't expect someone who looked like her to be cute and cuddly. Yet with this hulk of a man, she *felt* cuddly. He would be horrified if he knew her thoughts.

But Jesse showed no signs of horror. He leaned against the doorjamb. "Six o'clock, Shelby. Don't disappoint me."

The words stuck in her throat. She wet her lips. "You'd be relieved."

Jesse leaned down, and his lips brushed her own.

The touch of his warm breath against her face and the light kiss sent fingers of shivers up her spine. She had to get away from him before she disgraced herself. Scrambling back, she grabbed her key from her pocket and fumbled it into the lock.

"Shelby."

She didn't turn. "Don't worry, I'll be there. I won't jeopardize your precious trip."

"Why are you angry?"

"It's late, and I'm tired." She finally succeeded in unlocking the door and shoved it open. Stepping inside, she flipped on the light and turned to face him, now that she was safe inside.

"What are you afraid of now, Shelby? Me? Or is it life in general?"

There was no way she was going to touch that one. "Good night, Jesse."

His heavy sigh made her feel guilty, but she shut the door firmly. She just wasn't up to dealing with any more emotion tonight.

five

Jesse kicked off his shoes and jogged along the shore. Sunrise rimmed the eastern clouds with pink, but he didn't pause to enjoy the sight. His morning run was a ritual he'd begun when he was fifteen. He would miss it while they were at sea. His feet kicked up the sand behind him, and his measured breathing sounded nearly as loud as the pounding surf to his right. He was glad for the distraction.

Guilt ravaged him. He should have told Shelby the truth last night, but he'd been afraid she wouldn't come on the trip if she knew, and he couldn't allow that. This involved more than just himself and his burgeoning feelings for Shelby. He had to remember that. Not that she would believe he was attracted to her, not once she discovered the truth. Though he hadn't lied, he hadn't been open with her, either. Now he was caught in a tangled web, and he had to figure out a way to make sure she didn't talk to Palmer before they left.

Pushing his troubled thoughts away, he tried to pray, as he usually did when he ran, but God seemed far away this morning. It was his fault, not God's. His guilt had slammed a door between them. Sighing, he turned and jogged back to where he'd left his shoes. He might as well get to the *Jocelyn*. It was going to be a long day. Once they were out to sea, he could confess and get this crushing guilt off his chest.

Andy was already aboard when Jesse arrived. Dressed in ragged cutoffs, he was checking the rigging.

Jesse stepped over the coils of rope Andy was working on. "Anyone else here?"

"Just me and Heather. She's below putting bedding away. She took it all home last night and washed it."

"What did you think of Shelby?" Jesse kept his voice casual. If his best friend thought there was any real interest in Shelby as a woman, he would be humming the wedding march and making a general nuisance of himself.

"More vulnerable than she wants people to know. Tall, isn't she?"

Jesse huffed. "Tall and gorgeous." Too late, he realized he'd given himself away in his eagerness to defend her.

Andy began to grin. "Not too tall for someone six-six, is she?"

Much to Jesse's annoyance, Andy began to whistle the wedding march, just as Jesse had expected. He gritted his teeth. "Enough already. I'm not blind, but that doesn't mean I'm interested, either."

"That explains your hangdog look this morning. You're feeling guilty, aren't you? So, tell her the whole story."

Jesse sighed, but before he could answer, he saw the rest of the crew approaching in the inflatable dinghy. Shelby's hands gripped the sides. Her face was white, but determined. Jesse went to the rail and leaned over. "Want me to help you aboard?" he asked.

Shelby looked up. Her green eyes were wide and fearful, but she bit her lip and shook her head. "I can do it."

He felt like a cruel taskmaster as he watched her gather her courage and seize the ladder with trembling hands.

Hugging the ladder for a moment, she closed her eyes then climbed slowly. Jesse pulled her aboard as soon as she was within reach.

She pulled away almost immediately and straightened her shoulders. Dressed in no-nonsense jeans and a businesslike jacket, she presented a formidable figure, with her imposing height and brisk air. Jesse itched to punch beneath that pseudomasculine demeanor. He steered his thoughts away from that dangerous direction.

"I brought foodstuffs," she told him. "They're in the dinghy." She turned and looked back down, but her color went a decided green. "Can you get Scarlet?"

Jesse nodded and took the dog from Shelby's out-stretched hands. He yanked the bow from Scarlet's hair and dropped her to the deck. He then helped Brian bring the bags aboard. Much of the food was canned.

"I want to check on the amount of space I have before I buy any fresh or frozen food." Briskly, Shelby began to carry bags below.

Jesse followed her. "There's a small freezer section. We'll be able to fish, so that will be a main staple of our protein."

Shelby gazed about the small galley. Her pallor lessened as she inspected the stainless steel counters and small cabinets. A satisfied smile played about her lips, and Jesse could tell she was yearning to try her culinary skills.

"I'll put things away," she said.

He watched her move around the galley like she'd done it all her life. She planted her feet apart to balance herself against the rolling of the boat, and he suppressed a grin. For all her protests about not being a sailor, she was picking things up fast.

"I wish you wouldn't stare at me," Shelby snapped.

Heat rose in his neck. "I'll be topside when you're finished." He kept a rein on his temper and turned away before he said something he would regret. But he couldn't blame her. He *had* been staring. Self-disgust filled him. He was acting like a lovesick schoolboy. It was ridiculous, and he didn't know why she intrigued him. He'd seen attractive women before.

Twila raised one black eyebrow when he entered the navigation cabin. "You look like a bear someone woke up too early," she said. "What's got you so riled?"

"Nothing. I'm fine." He flipped open the logbook and didn't meet her gaze.

"Uh-huh, I can see that."

His lips twitched at the disbelief in her voice. She was always able to get around him. Her nickname, "Mom," was well-deserved. "That woman is driving me crazy." He sat on the seat and pulled the logbook toward him.

Twila gave a throaty chuckle. "Child, you aren't the first man I've heard say that about a woman." She pointed her finger at him. "Don't you hurt her, Jesse. She's like a wounded doe with those big, scared eyes."

Andy thrust his head in the door. "Looks like we're all here. Let's get ready to shove off."

Jesse was only too happy to oblige. He didn't want to tell Twila it was already too late—Shelby would be hurt when she discovered he hadn't been open with her.

❦

With Jesse gone, Shelby's shoulders relaxed. Why had he been staring? She was no debutante fluffette. Men didn't stare at women like her. And she preferred that they didn't.

It had been uncomfortable. She didn't like to be in the spotlight.

Humming, she tucked cans and plastic containers of pasta in every nook and cranny she could find. At the grocery store a helpful clerk had told her not to take anything aboard in cardboard, since it harbored bugs. She put her notebook filled with recipes into the cabinet and went topside.

Heather gave her a welcoming smile. "You're looking better. What did you do to Jesse? He came stomping through here like he was trying to squash something nasty on the floor."

Turning her hot cheeks away, Shelby avoided answering. "Did he tell you I'll be doing all the cooking?"

Heather clapped her hands. "You mean, no more of Jesse's macaroni and cheese? That's all he ever fixed. It was always rubbery with too much salt."

Shelby burst into laughter. "You don't like macaroni and cheese? Jesse said you weren't picky."

"I love it, just not Jesse's. You'd have to taste it to believe it."

"Was that my name I heard?" Jesse strolled toward them. He didn't seem at all discomfited by their earlier disagreement.

"I was thanking Shelby for saving me from your cooking," Heather said with an impertinent poke at Jesse's stomach.

He flinched automatically. "How do you know Shelby's is any better?"

"I can tell by looking. Anyone who appears as competent as Shelby is good at whatever she does," Heather said. "Is it time for lunch yet?"

Shelby laughed. Why couldn't she handle men as easily as other women did? Heather obviously was a master at it.

Twila joined them. "Are you hasslin' this child?"

"No," Heather and Jesse chorused.

Twila tucked her hand into Shelby's arm. "Come with Twila, Child. I'll protect you. It's my watch at the helm. I'll show you how to tell which way the wind is blowin'."

"Will your instruments tell me which way Jesse is blowing?" Shelby asked as soon as they were out of earshot.

Twila laughed. "That's easy, Child. Just watch him. When he tugs on his ear, he's tryin' to think of how he can say yes to your request without lookin' like a wimp. If he rests his chin on his hand with one finger reachin' up to his eye, he's already got his mind made up and is just tryin' to let you down easy. Rubbin' his forehead means he's tired and tryin' not to take it out on you, so if he spouts off then, don't take it personally."

"You've known him a long time." Shelby wished she could ask her what kind of woman he liked and whether he dated much.

Twila gestured for her to be seated at the seat in front of the instrument panel in the navigation room. "Forever, Child. I taught that boy how to sail back when he was fifteen, and I was twenty. Seems like a long time ago. His mama was still alive then." She tilted her head to one side and considered Shelby. "You know, you kind of remind me of her. Maybe that's why Jesse is so smitten."

"Smitten?" Shelby clamped her teeth together, but it was too late—the word was already hanging in the air.

Twila patted her hand. "Trust your instincts, Child. You've seen the way he looks at you. Like you were that last piece of chocolate pie he's hankerin' after."

Shelby decided it was time to change the subject. Twila was merely trying to make her feel better. She'd obviously seen Shelby's own attraction to the handsome Jesse. "What was his mother like?"

"Oh, my, she was like the sea herself. Bein' around Molly was like sittin' beside the ocean for an afternoon. When you left her, you felt cleansed and renewed. She was tall and serene, like you."

Shelby wanted to laugh. No one had ever called her serene. Maybe she was better at hiding her inner turmoil than she thought. Still, the fact that Jesse's mother had been tall was comforting. Maybe he wasn't as put off by that fact as most men were.

"There was one difference, though," Twila said in a reflective voice. "She wasn't ashamed of being a woman."

A warm flush crept up Shelby's neck. "I'm not ashamed of being a woman!"

Twila sniffed. "Look at that outfit you're wearin'. It looks like a man's jacket. And you always scrape your gorgeous hair back in a clip. I'm just surprised you haven't chopped it all off. I'm goin' to have to take you in hand this trip, Child. It's time you realized you're a woman, and a lovely one at that."

The heat in Shelby's face intensified. "I'm not lovely," she burst out. "I've never even had a serious boyfriend, Twila."

"And whose fault is that? I would venture to guess that you've been asked out, but your height bothered you more than it ever did any man."

Shelby was silent a moment. "I've never been asked out by a man taller than me," she admitted.

Twila's southern accent thickened. "You think he has to be taller to be able to love you? Children have some of the most powerful love in the world, but they're no bigger than a minute. Open your heart, Child. Don't close yourself off until someone comes along who meets your narrow notion of looks. Looks fade." She tapped Shelby's chest. "What you are inside is what's important. Look at the inner man."

She turned around, and her tone became brisk and businesslike. "Now let's get to work so you can earn that business suit you're wearin'."

Shelby's thought whirled as she tried to pay attention to Twila's explanation of the instruments. Was Twila right? Was she more bothered by her height than the men she met? She tried to remember the last time a man had asked her out. It had been Todd Langley, six months ago. He was about five-ten, three inches shorter than she was. She'd taken one look at his small, narrow feet and turned him down. She wasn't about to date a man with a shoe size smaller than her own.

And she still wasn't, no matter what Twila said. Maybe it was shallow, but she wasn't interested in a man who didn't make her feel like a woman. She didn't want to think about Jesse's towering height and his strong-jawed face. When he was around, she felt every inch a woman, and she wasn't sure she liked the sensation, for all her protestations to herself about wanting a "real man."

Scarlet whined at her feet, and Shelby picked her up. She'd stick with her dog. Scarlet made no demands on her except for a place to sleep, food to eat, and an occasional cuddle. She didn't care if Shelby wore a size eleven shoe— she only cared that her hands were gentle and loving.

"I'd better go fix lunch," she told Twila.

Twila brightened. "I heard you were takin' over that little chore for all of us. We're to be spared Jesse's macaroni and cheese."

Shelby burst into laughter. "It must *really* be bad. I already heard about it from Heather."

Twila shook her head. "Child, you have no idea."

"I'll try to fix a good lunch to dispel any recollection of Jesse's cooking," Shelby promised.

"It will have to be mighty good to make me forget that mess of sticky goo," Twila said with a visible shudder.

"Just wait and see. I have quite a treat planned for you." Shelby carried Scarlet below deck, then put her down. Humming, she began to pull the ingredients from the refrigerator and the cabinets. This was one place she was in her element.

She took out the chicken salad she'd made last night and put lettuce on plates, then added a scoop of chicken salad to each one. Whipping up a fruit salad, she set the table and put the fruit salad in the center. When everything was ready, she stepped to the ladder leading to the deck and called the crew to lunch.

Jesse's eyes widened when he came down into the galley. Brian was right behind him, and he whistled softly.

Heather hugged Shelby. "I love chicken salad! It looks scrumptious. Can I get drinks?"

"There's pink lemonade in the refrigerator if anyone wants it," Shelby said.

"I do!" Jesse spoke first, but the others joined the chorus of assents.

Heather poured the lemonade, and they all sat at the

table. Shelby was gratified to see that they bowed their heads as though prayer was something they were used to. She was startled to see derision cross Brian's face, but he obediently bowed his head as well.

Jesse cleared his throat and spoke clearly. "Lord, we thank You for this delicious food before us. Thank You for sending Shelby to us, and bless her as she works among us. Help us all to shine Your light to the world. In Jesus' name, amen."

"Amen," Andy echoed. "Now let's eat!"

Shelby relaxed as they all declared it the best luncheon they'd ever had. Every speck of food was gone before Jesse pushed back from the table.

"I could give you a break tomorrow and fix my famous macaroni and cheese," he said.

"No, please!" Twila held up her hands. "Did you have to mention that horror? Shelby promised I would forget it, and I did. Now you've gone and spoiled it."

Jesse laughed. "Shelby did the cooking, the least one of us could do is help her clean up. Any takers?"

"I will," Brian said.

Shelby nearly groaned aloud, but she managed a smile. "It won't take long," she told Brian.

He shrugged, and his blue-eyed gaze followed her as she began to put the condiments away. "I don't mind. Saves me from fighting with the ropes."

Shelby glanced at his feet. A size twelve at least. And he was about her height. She realized where her thoughts had taken her and turned away, heat scorching her cheeks. Brian smiled, and she realized with a sick feeling in her stomach that he thought the color in her cheeks was from his nearness. Moving away, she turned the water on in the sink and began washing the dishes. The sooner this ordeal was over, the better. She'd tell Jesse she preferred to clean up by herself.

Searching for a topic of conversation, she kept her tone light and impersonal. "What do you do, Brian? When you're not undertaking a voyage like this, that is."

"I do lots of things," Brian said. "I've been a professional fisherman, a welder, and a well-rigger. But I like sailing the best. I earn enough money to live on, then find a boat heading to sea and offer my services. I love the ocean." His voice was low and passionate.

Shelby shivered. She would never understand this love of the sea that men had. The ocean was fearsome and strange to her.

"You're going to need someone to help you run the charter business when we get back," he said in a matter-of-fact voice. "I'd like to apply for the job."

So that was his real interest. She should have known it wasn't her fair self he found so alluring. A laugh almost bubbled up, but she caught it just in time.

"I'll keep that in mind," she said gravely. "I haven't decided what I'm going to do yet."

He nodded. "You've got time. We'll be gone six to eight months, most likely."

Six to eight months. Shelby's heart sank. As long as she was here in the galley she was content, but this afternoon she had to begin to learn to work the sails and halyards. The thought frightened her, but she pushed the fear away. One day at a time. She would deal with her fear moment by moment, and with God's help, she would conquer it.

six

Shelby glanced at her watch. The illuminated dial glowed in the dark. Nearly eight o'clock. She had missed her date with Palmer, but she wasn't really unhappy about that. It had been a grueling day, and she was in no mood for chitchat. Her muscles ached from pulling on the lines, and her hands were raw from tying knots in the rough ropes. But a sense of satisfaction spread a warm glow over her aches and pains. Jesse had commended her work, and the entire crew had been complimentary of her cooking.

Scarlet whined at her feet, and she picked her up and cuddled her. "I've neglected you today, haven't I? And you've been such a good girl." She'd taught the little dog to use a litter box when she was still a puppy, but she hadn't been too sure how well she would do onboard the boat. Everyone seemed enamored of Scarlet. Everyone except Jesse. He took the bow out of Scarlet's hair every time he saw her, but Shelby kept putting it back in.

Still carrying the dog, she climbed the ladder to the deck. Jesse was leaning against the railing, watching the waves.

She stopped back from the rail a few feet. "Are we almost back to the dock? I hope you realize you've kept me out too long; Palmer probably wonders what happened to me."

A strange expression sped across his face, but it was

gone so quickly she wasn't sure what it was. Could it have been relief? She told herself she was imagining things. He'd been distant and businesslike today, making no reference to their camaraderie last night. And certainly no repeat of that kiss.

He shrugged. "Just as well; Palmer would bore you to death."

"How do you know Palmer?" At the question, his shoulders seemed to tense, and her curiosity was piqued even further.

"I've seen him around."

He didn't seem eager to reveal any details. "Why do I get the feeling you don't like him?"

Jesse moved restlessly. "Guys like Palmer are all alike. They think the world owes them something and that they're a cut above the rest of us mere mortals. He takes what he wants with no regard for others. He's determined to win this race no matter who he hurts."

The tinge of bitterness in his voice startled her. This seemed personal, not just the passing view about an acquaintance. Before she could ask any more questions, he abruptly changed the subject.

"We leave tomorrow around noon. That will give you time to get the rest of your foodstuffs bought and your packing done."

"Tomorrow! I thought we had one more day." She felt as though she couldn't breathe. The thought of being able to step ashore in a few hours was all that had gotten her through some of her worst moments today.

His gaze softened. "You're ready, Shelby. Once we're actually on our way, you'll settle down. The rest of the crew are itching to get started, and there's no reason to wait any longer. They've all agreed that you're ready. Besides, there's a storm heading this way, and I want to try to outrun it."

She wasn't ready to face a storm or anything else. Forcing herself to take a deep breath, she swallowed and ran her fingers through Scarlet's silky fur. Running the verse about fear through her mind again, she sent up a quick prayer for strength. She'd given her word to this course, and she had to go through with it.

"I'll have to let my lawyer and my family know."

He nodded. "Don't look so scared. This will be the trip of a lifetime. You'll never forget it."

"I'm more worried about surviving it," she said with a wry grin.

He stepped a bit closer, and her mouth went dry. Brushing his knuckles across her chin, he gazed into her eyes. "I won't let anything happen to you," he said in a low voice.

Noisy laughter interrupted the kiss Shelby was sure had been about to happen. Dragging her gaze away, she took a step back, trying not to let him see her disappointment.

"There you are, Child." Twila had her arm around Heather as they approached. "We're tryin' to divvy up the private quarters. Heather wants to hog the nice cabin for her and Andy, but since you own the boat, I think you should have it. With me as a bunkie, of course."

"I've already decided to put Shelby in the captain's cabin," Jesse said. "Heather, you and Andy can have the other private cabin. It's almost as big as the captain's cabin. Brian and I will take the bunks in the main salon." He gazed at Shelby. "Do you mind sharing the cabin with Twila?"

"Of course not," Shelby said. "But we could take the smaller one and let Andy and Heather take the one with its own head." She was proud she remembered the nautical term for toilet.

"I was just teasing," Heather said quickly. "Besides, Twila is bigger than me. She needs the larger cabin."

Twila sniffed and patted her own mocha-colored arm. "Least I got some color, Child, instead of lookin' like a pale stick of mozzarella cheese like some people."

Shelby giggled at their lighthearted joking. Glancing at Jesse out of the corner of her eye, she saw his grin widen. She dragged her attention back to Twila. "Do you snore, Twila? Should I buy earplugs?"

"You weren't supposed to ask that yet," Heather said. "We didn't want to scare you off."

Twila put her hands on her hips. "This child won't believe your lies about me."

"If you gals are done ragging on one another, you've got work to do tonight," Jesse broke in. "We're ready to dock. Be back here at noon sharp tomorrow."

Shelby's steps lagged as she walked from the dock up to the house. The front porch glowed with a welcoming light, and her spirits lifted. When the voyage got long, if she could just keep in mind her home waiting for her, she might be able to make it.

The answering machine was blinking when she laid her purse on the hall table. She pushed the play button.

Palmer's voice came on. "Hi, Shelby. What happened? I came by to pick you up, and no one answered the door. Call when you get in. I haven't eaten yet, and we can take in a late dinner."

Great. Just what she didn't want to do. Well, she would just call him and bow out. He would understand when he heard they were leaving tomorrow. Kicking off her shoes, she went to the living room and found the portable phone. Before she called Palmer, she called her mother.

"Hi, Mom, I just wanted to let you know I'm leaving on the voyage a day sooner than we planned. How have you been feeling?"

Her mother's voice sounded firm and steady, and Shelby felt her heart lighten with relief. "Fine, Sweetheart. The new medicine seems to be helping, and I'm not even having to use the walker right now."

"That's great, Mom! Have you made your plane reservation yet?"

"My flight arrives next Friday. I made a reservation with a limo service to get me to the house like you suggested. Did Palmer get ahold of you? He called here asking if I'd heard from you. I'm glad you're going out with him tonight. He seems to be a nice young man."

There went her plans to pack and go to bed. . . . "I'm going to be calling him in a few minutes. We're having dinner."

"So he said. I'm glad you've found a young man to squire you around already."

Shelby nearly sighed at the hope in her mother's voice. "Don't get any ideas, Mom."

"I worry about you, Shelby. This trip will be good for you. You've been in a rut, a rut of your own making. It's about time you realized how lovely you really are. Palmer seemed very interested."

Shelby rolled her eyes. "It's just dinner, Mom. I'm going

to be gone for six months."

"He may still be available when you get back."

Shelby sighed, and her mother's tone softened. "Sorry, Shelby. I'll try not to push. Be careful, Sweetheart. I'll miss you."

A lump formed in Shelby's throat. "I'll miss you, too, Mom. When I get back, we'll have our own place, and no one will ever be able to take it away from us. Do any redecorating you want while I'm gone." Since Shelby's father had deserted them when she was five, her mother had struggled to feed and clothe them both. This was Shelby's chance to pay her back for all the sacrifices her mother had made. She wished she could be there to watch her mom's reaction when she first saw the house. She would probably cry.

Shelby reluctantly looked up Palmer's number and dialed it. "Sorry I missed you, Palmer. The boat got in late. We're leaving tomorrow, so we have to make it an early evening."

"Tomorrow?" Palmer's voice rose in alarm. "Um, I have something I really need to talk to you about before you go. We can have a quick bite at the Blue Onion, just down the road from your house. I'll be there in fifteen minutes."

He hung up, and Shelby put the phone down thoughtfully. There was a firm hint of determination in his voice. Whatever it was, it must be important.

She barely had time to wash up and make herself presentable with fresh makeup by the time the doorbell rang. Palmer was smiling and handsome when she opened the door. His gray blazer and tweed slacks were flawlessly pressed and perfectly tailored. His blond hair was a smooth, shining cap on his head.

A perfect picture of masculinity. Shelby smiled. "It's a bit chilly. Let me get my jacket." She grabbed her jacket from the hall closet and followed Palmer to the car. A Mercedes sedan, black as ebony and just as expensive. It fit with what she'd noticed about its owner; he was a trifle arrogant and proud of his status.

He drove sedately to the restaurant, and Shelby couldn't help comparing tonight's ride with last night's. She knew no amount of coaxing would convince Palmer to slam his foot on the gas pedal the way Jesse had last night.

Pushing the memory away, she struggled for a safe topic of conversation. "Mom told me you called her. I can't tell you how much I appreciate your making her feel welcome."

He gave a self-deprecating shrug. "Well, we are all family. Sort of. That's the other reason I had to talk to you tonight. I feel an obligation to make sure you know the truth."

"What truth?" His sober expression filled her with trepidation.

"About Jesse Titus." His lip curled with contempt when he said the name.

Maybe she was about to find out where the animosity between Jesse and Palmer came from. She wasn't sure she wanted to know.

❦

Jesse paced his small hotel room. The tight confines were already getting on his nerves, but it wasn't just the temporary housing. Trust. That was one thing he found difficult to achieve, and his present situation was just another indication of that. He should have trusted God and told Shelby the entire truth.

His sea chest was packed, and all was in readiness for tomorrow, except for one thing. He had to tell Shelby everything. His deception was tearing at his insides like the sharp teeth of remorse. There was no way he could let her get onboard that boat in the morning without knowing the truth. She would probably hate him, and he couldn't blame her.

In sudden decision, he grabbed his jacket and opened the door. She was probably home packing. Even if she backed out after hearing what he had to say, he had to be honest. Would she forgive him? It didn't seem likely, and the thought deeply grieved Jesse. He cared about Shelby more than he wanted to admit to himself.

It was too chilly to have the top down tonight, and the closeness of the airless car interior added to his trepidation at the thought of confessing to Shelby. He pulled into Shelby's driveway and parked. Walking to the door, he rang the bell. Scarlet yapped inside, and he pounded on the door. When there was no answer, he finally turned to go back to the car.

The smooth purr of a powerful car came up the road. Pausing with his hand on the car latch, he turned to look as a black Mercedes pulled in behind him. His heart sank. It looked like Palmer's car. Moments later, Palmer opened the door, and Jesse's shoulders slumped when Shelby got out of the passenger side.

"Jesse." Her voice was taut and cold.

The wounded gaze she wore told him he was too late.

"You've been busted, Titus," Palmer sneered. "I'm appalled at the way you've deceived this dear young woman."

"Did you tell her the whole story, Wilson? What about

your part in this whole mess?" Jesse asked quietly. "Did you tell her you sank my boat?"

Palmer laughed, but the mirth rang unconvincingly in Jesse's ears. Did Shelby hear that same insincerity? Somehow, Jesse doubted it.

"Don't try to drag me down to your level, Titus. You've already proved just how truthful you are. Not much of a Christian, are you?"

Jesse winced. "You're right, Palmer, and I came here to tell Shelby the truth."

"I don't want to hear anything you have to say," Shelby said as she brushed by him. She dug through her purse in jerky movements. Finding her key, she rammed it into the lock and pushed open the door. Palmer started to follow her, but she held up a hand. "I don't want to appear ungrateful, Palmer, but I've had all I can take tonight."

Palmer scowled, then gave an obviously forced smile. "Very well, Shelby. I'll call you tomorrow. Perhaps we can have a more leisurely dinner." He gave Jesse an insolent smile and strolled to his car. The engine roared to life, and he backed out the driveway.

The hurt in Shelby's face tore at Jesse's composure. He had to tell her the full story. Palmer would certainly shade things to look as bad as possible. She began to shut the door, but he stuck his foot in it.

"Please, Shelby; I know it looks bad, but let me explain."

Tears shimmered on her lashes, and she blinked furiously. "I trusted you, Jesse. I feel like such a fool. What was that kiss all about—did you feel I needed a bit more persuasion?"

"No, Shelby, I kissed you because I wanted to kiss you."

Jesse stiffened his shoulders. If that's how she really thought of him, there was no more to say.

She laughed, and the bitterness of it shocked him. He was just beginning to sense how deeply she was hurt.

"I initially had no intention of following through on your uncle's will," he began.

She held up a hand. "Stop, please. I can't take any more tonight."

"You have to hear the truth."

"Now you're eager to tell the truth, but where was that eagerness three days ago? You used me, Jesse. I don't know what to believe of anything you've told me."

Jesse took a deep breath and brushed past her. She stood in the doorway a moment then slowly followed him inside.

"Didn't you hear me? I want you to go, Jesse. Let's talk about this tomorrow when we're both calmer." She held the door open, but when he held his ground, she sighed and shut the door. "I need some tea if you're going to force me to listen to your paltry excuses. Do you want a cup?"

"No, thanks." He followed her to the kitchen with Scarlet on his heels.

Shelby filled the kettle with water and set it on the stove. She took a yellow teapot down from the shelf and put two tea bags in it. The silence in the kitchen stretched between them, and Jesse jumped when the teakettle began to shriek. Shelby poured the water into the teapot and placed it on a tray bearing a cup. Picking up the tray, she brushed by Jesse and headed toward the living room. Jesse followed slowly, marshaling his thoughts.

There were dark circles under Shelby's green eyes, and Jesse's guilt increased. He was the cause of that strain he saw on her face.

She sat on the sofa and poured a cup of tea. "Let's get it over with," she said, curling her feet under her.

Jesse sat in the chair opposite her. "When the lawyer told me the provisions of the will, I laughed. I told him to forget it, that I wasn't interested in baby-sitting a spoiled little rich girl."

Her eyes widened, and tears flooded them. She ducked her head and took a sip of tea.

"He pressed me to take my copy of the papers, and I left his office. When I got home, my father phoned, and I'd never heard him sound so desperate. The bank had called. He had managed to talk them into a six-month extension of the loan, but if we didn't pay at the end of that time, we would lose the resort. I couldn't let that happen to my father. He had poured his whole life into Coral Reef. He'd taken out the loan for me to enter the race, and I couldn't let him suffer for it. I was confident I could win the race, but if I didn't, my father would lose everything."

Shelby bit her lip. "That doesn't justify deceiving me."

"I never lied to you, Shelby. I just didn't tell you the full story."

"It amounted to same thing. Half a truth is the same as a lie."

"I realize that now. I had never fully appreciated it before. Anyway, I looked at that copy of the will in my hand. It said that if Palmer and I both enter the race, the winner would receive two hundred thousand dollars. And if I could take Lloyd's niece around the Horn, I would inherit one hundred thousand dollars, enough to pay back the bank even if I didn't win the race."

"So I was merely insurance. If you win the race, you won't need to help me overcome my fear of the water. If you lose, I'm your ace in the hole." Shelby no longer sounded angry, just drained and weary.

"Did Palmer tell you the rest of what is in the will?" Jesse asked. "If you don't go around the Horn, the loser gets your inheritance. I stand to gain more if you stay home. Think about that before you chuck all you've learned the past two days."

Shelby's eyes widened. "No, he neglected to tell me that." She sounded perilously near tears. "Though I'm not sure why that hurts now. He's just using me for his own purposes like you've been doing." She took a deep breath. "But it doesn't matter. I'm not quitting now. I don't understand why Uncle Lloyd put such crazy provisions in his will, but I'm not letting either you or Palmer get the best of me. I'm not giving up my home, not for you or Palmer."

She stood abruptly. "I'd like you to leave now, Jesse."

He rose slowly. "Shelby, I know I've hurt you—"

"No more, Jesse," she interrupted. "I'll see you tomorrow at noon, but I want it understood that our relationship is strictly business from this moment on."

His heart sank. The more he saw her, the more he was drawn to her, but his deception had ruined it all. It was a bitter pill to swallow.

seven

Tears burned Shelby's eyes, and her throat was raw from swallowing her pain. But she held her head high as she shut the door behind him. She should have known better. Every man she had ever known had betrayed her, starting with her father's desertion when she was five. Letting her guard down around Jesse had been a mistake, one she regretted now with bitter intensity.

Scarlet sensed her pain and whined at her feet. When Shelby picked up the dog, Scarlet licked her chin anxiously, and at last Shelby let the tears fall. In spite of all her brave words, she was tempted to pack her bags and head to the airport. Bolstering her flagging courage, she shook her head.

"They won't get the best of me, Scarlet," she whispered through the tears streaming down her cheeks. "They'd both like nothing better than for me to turn tail and run. But I won't let them win. I'm used to fighting on my own. I'm going to pack, but it will be for the voyage. I'll get through the next few months, then we'll all have our own home, our own place."

Place was very important to Shelby. After her father left them, they had lived in one ratty apartment after another, all the same except for the address. They had all smelled of stale cigarette smoke and other people's dirt, no matter how much her mother scrubbed. That was why she was so driven in her career, so she could provide a place for her mother. Here was that place, that home. Here she smelled the clean scent of the sea, not the acrid stench of defeat and abandonment. She couldn't let it all slip away.

"I'm going to need Your help, Lord," she whispered. "I can't do this alone. Help me to keep my dignity and take this fear from me." She dropped Scarlet on the floor and went to the kitchen. Fixing another pot of tea—her first pot had cooled before she could drink it—she carried it to her room, then curled up on the bed with her Bible and read until calmness seeped back into her soul. God would never let her down, though men always would. And that was all that mattered.

She packed her things into her uncle's sea chest, then went to bed. The next morning her eyes felt gritty, but when she stared in the mirror, she saw no trace of her pain and disillusionment. She was a bit pale, but as a redhead, that was a common occurrence. A bit of makeup would fix that. When she was ready, she walked around the house one last time. She hated to leave this place where she felt safe and whole, but her mother would be here in a few days. When Shelby returned in a few months, they could begin their new life. The thought comforted her.

Brian and Andy arrived early to take the sea chest and the groceries to the boat. While they hauled everything down to the dock, she took Scarlet and made sure the doors were locked and the windows closed. She had arranged for the car rental agency to pick up the car, so she left the keys under the seat and locked the car. The adventure was about to begin.

Shelby's heart roared in her ears as she walked down to

the dock. The sea seemed menacing to her this morning, whipped by the wind and as gray as the low-hanging clouds overhead. She didn't want to see Jesse this morning, but she had no choice. Stepping into the inflatable dinghy, she sat in the bow with Scarlet on her lap. The sea spray struck her in the face and left a salt tang on her lips. She stared straight ahead as the boat loomed closer. This would be her home for the next several months. The thought terrified her.

"You okay?" Heather shouted above the pounding waves.

Shelby nodded. "Is this the storm Jesse talked about?"

Heather shook her head. "It's still offshore, but the sea is a little choppy because of it."

A little choppy? Shelby's heart sank.

Heather grinned. "Don't look so scared," she called. "We'll be out of it soon."

"Yeah, but why do I think there will be others?" Shelby said.

"You'll have found your sea legs by then." Heather gave her another encouraging grin.

The boat drew closer, and Shelby saw Jesse's broad shoulders onboard. Her heart heaved in her chest with the boat's pitch, but she knew it wasn't because of the waves. She didn't quite know what to say to Jesse or how to act. Straightening her shoulders, she composed her face into an indifferent mask. She wouldn't let him know just how much he had hurt her. Their relationship had been just beginning, anyway. It shouldn't have hurt as much as it did.

Jesse came to the ladder as the dinghy moored beside the boat. His dark eyes sought her face, and Shelby gave him an impersonal nod. The worried crease between his eyes smoothed, and he nodded back. Shelby wondered if he hadn't been sure she would show up. She was his insurance in case he lost the race.

Gritting her teeth, she tried to ignore the waves splashing over the side of the dinghy and stood to clamber up the ladder. She zipped Scarlet into her jacket and grasped the ladder. The waves slapped at her feet, but she scampered up the ladder before she was too wet. Jesse grasped her arm, and she jerked away, almost toppling back into the water below. The sharp taste of fear on her tongue, she grabbed at his arm, and he hauled her aboard.

"Thank you," she said and jerked away without looking into his eyes. Trust her to make a complete fool of herself. Her heart still pounding from the near disaster, she turned away from him. "I'll take my things below."

"I've already stowed them in your cabin, but I didn't get the groceries put away yet," Jesse said.

She ignored the placating tone in his voice. "I'll do it." Carrying Scarlet, she hurried below deck. She put the dog into her cabin. Scarlet would have to stay below in choppy seas like this. Glancing around the cabin, she noticed that Jesse had put her sea chest at the foot of the bed. The bunks were neatly made up, and a Boyd bear sat in the middle of the bed. There was a bow around its neck, and a card.

Shelby smiled and picked up the bear. Hugging its softness, she flipped the card over.

"CAN YOU FORGIVE ME?" it read. It was from Jesse. Tears stung her eyes, and she blinked them away, furious at her own weakness. Though she was tempted to throw his gift back at him, she knew it would be churlish. And she loved Boyd bears. She sighed and set the bear back on the bed. She would have to thank him graciously, though the words might choke her.

Her gaze strayed back to the card. Forgiveness. She wasn't acting much like a Christian where he was concerned, was she? Picking up the bear again, she hugged it against her chest and went to find Jesse. She had to let go of this anger and hurt. He was nothing to her. She would forgive him and put it behind her.

The rest of the crew were busy on deck. Jesse was in the navigation cabin, and his eyes widened when she stepped inside. He gave her an uncertain smile when he saw the bear in her arms.

She smiled back and walked to him. "Thank you," she said.

"Does that mean I'm forgiven?" he asked. His dark eyes studied her face intently.

She dropped her gaze. "I'll try," she said.

He touched her arm. "I never meant to hurt you, Shelby. Can we start over?"

As friends, that's all he meant, she thought. She bit her lip and held out her hand. "Friends," she said.

He hesitated then took her hand. "Friends," he echoed softly.

The touch of his hand did funny things to her insides. The less time she spent around him, the better. She didn't know if she could ever be just friends with him when her heart longed for much more. But she couldn't let him see that.

She smiled distantly and stepped toward the door. "I'd better get my kitchen in order. Are we shoving off soon?"

"In about fifteen minutes. I want all the crew topside for that."

"It won't take long to stow the food."

He nodded and turned back to his navigational charts. Shelby went to the ladder and down to the galley below. Twila was already at work putting things away.

She smiled when she saw Shelby. "Why, Child, you have a face as long as a cat's tail. You that scared about leavin' on this old boat?"

Shelby managed a smile. "I'm fine. Looks like you've done most of the work."

Twila's shrewd gaze lingered on Shelby's face, but she merely nodded. "I don't want to risk anything breakin'. I've been just imaginin' all those fine meals you're goin' to cook."

"Hey, you two," Andy called down the hatch. "We're ready to shove off. Jesse wants us all up here."

Twila shoved the last Tupperware container of cereal into the cupboard and latched it. "The adventure is about to begin." Her voice was gay, and she linked arms with Shelby. "Smile, Child. This will be a trip you won't ever forget."

That was an understatement. Shelby smiled and followed Twila up the ladder. The crew was assembled near the rigging.

Jesse glanced around, then nodded. "Looks like we're all here. I want to pray for a safe voyage before we get started."

Shelby saw the look of derision on Brian's face, but he obediently bowed his head like the rest of them. Her gaze caught Jesse's for a moment, then she closed her eyes.

"Lord, You are the maker and keeper of the deep. We ask for Your guidance and strong arm of protection as we undertake this voyage. Keep us all safe and put the wind in our sails and the currents at our back. We commit our keeping into Your hands. In Jesus' name, amen."

"Amen," Shelby and Twila echoed.

Jesse smiled. "Let's hoist sail."

The men cheered as Jesse went to the controls. He fired the engine, and the boat motored slowly. Andy and Brian pulled on the halyard while Heather fed the luff into the groove. Twila worked the winch. The white sail unfurled and rose into position.

Pride and fear fought for possession of Shelby's chest and left her breathless with anticipation. Within minutes they were moving out to sea. She helped Heather secure the halyards with a cleat hitch, then coiled the lines. With all the sails raised, the boat quickly moved out to sea, and soon the sight of land was swallowed up in gray sky and sea.

The day sped by. Shelby kept busy helping trim the sails. Supper seemed somehow festive as the crew's high spirits spilled over into laughter and joking. By the time bedtime rolled around, Shelby had begun to relax. She didn't want to go to the deck in the dark, though, so she was glad her duties included cooking and cleanup. She dreaded having to take her turn at night watch. The black night and even blacker water terrified her. But at least her turn wouldn't be tonight. Jesse had promised to wait two or three days until she was more comfortable before assigning her a watch, but it was only fair that she take her turn.

At nine she went to the cabin. The boat pitched with the waves, and the cabin seemed claustrophobic. Twila was already in her pajamas and sitting on her bunk with her Bible in her lap.

She looked up when Shelby entered. "Well, Child, this is your first night aboard ship. Before long you'll wonder how you ever slept without the boat rockin' you like a cradle."

Shelby grimaced. "It will be a long time before that ever happens," she said. "I like things stationary and safe."

Twila gave a throaty laugh. "You'll see, Child. You'll see."

Shelby smiled and went to the head. Washing her face, she slipped into sweats and braided her hair to keep it from tangling in the night. She went back to their cabin and crawled into bed.

"Would you like us to pray together at night when we can?" Twila asked as she closed her Bible.

"I'd like that." Contentment washed over Shelby. God had arranged things well so far, and she was confident He would continue to do so.

The next few days passed quickly. The *Jocelyn* sped toward Ensenado, where the race would begin. Slowly, Shelby began to relax. She no longer jumped in terror at every slap of the waves against the hull, and she managed to walk on deck without a death grip on the rail or other parts of the boat. She kept her demeanor around Jesse cool and impersonal. Several times she saw him eye her uncertainly, but he never challenged her on her behavior.

As they sailed into Ensenado, the thrill of the race began to surge through her. Other white sails dotted the harbor, and the excitement among *Jocelyn*'s crew was almost palpable. Other motor/sailing yachts looked newer than their boat, but Shelby had confidence in Jesse and the rest of the crew. She wondered which boat was Palmer's.

"How about dinner at Amigos tonight?" Jesse asked as the crew assembled on deck to dock. "My dad will be expecting us."

Shelby picked up Scarlet. "Your dad?"

He nodded. "Our resort is here." He pointed to a cluster of buildings with a green and white flag waving over one low-slung building.

Shelby studied the resort. The buildings could use new shingles and paint, but the beach was lovely. Jesse maneuvered the boat to the dock, and a tall man with graying hair and Jesse's dark eyes hurried toward them. He had to be Jesse's father.

His gaze sought his son's form, and the smile on his face widened. "You made it, Son. I was beginning to worry. The race starts the day after tomorrow." He held out a hand and helped them all onto the dock. "Your brothers have planned quite a feast."

Jesse grinned. "I could smell it clear out to sea."

His father greeted the rest of the crew, then turned to Shelby. "Who's this lovely lady?"

"This is Shelby West," Jesse said. "Shelby, this old sea dog is my father, Mason Titus."

Mason took her hand and lifted it to his lips. "My son said you were beautiful, and so you are," he said. He scratched Scarlet's head, and she wiggled in delight.

"Jesse obviously inherited his smooth tongue from his father." Shelby smiled weakly and tried to hide her fluster. Her gaze shot to Jesse, but he merely folded his arms across his chest and grinned at her. Had he really mentioned her to his father? It seemed so.

Mason sent an amused glance toward Jesse. "My son has never before been accused of having a smooth tongue," he said. "He's usually much too blunt."

"I can smell that shrimp from here," Jesse put in. "We're starved."

Shelby's lips twitched at the uncomfortable expression on his face. She was much more eager to hear more about Jesse than she was to eat, but she followed the crew down the dock to the resort. Close up, it was even more dilapidated than it looked from the water. The buildings were weathered and in sore need of paint. Inside the restaurant, the wooden floorboards were sand-scoured and gray with age. But there was a charm and patina about the place that drew her. She could imagine how it would look with some sprucing up and a fresh coat of stain and polyurethane on the floor.

"Boys, your brother is here!" called Mason, shutting the door behind him.

Three men came through the door to the kitchen. They were all as tall as Jesse. They rushed to their brother, and amid the hugs and slaps on the back, Shelby tried to stay out of the way. Jesse introduced them.

"This is Aaron; he's the oldest and the bane of my life," Jesse said.

"Only because someone has to keep you in line," Aaron said. His hair was as black as Jesse's but straight, whereas Jesse's was curly. He had heavy black brows over his dark eyes.

"Kane is the philosopher of the family." Jesse pointed out the brother with blond hair and a gentle air about him. A thin scar arched over one eye like a pale eyebrow.

"And Brice is the baby in the family and spoiled rotten," Jesse said about the young man with sandy brown hair and freckles. He looked like a choirboy, except for the impish expression in his green eyes.

Those green eyes widened. "I call," he said.

The other three brothers groaned.

"You're a little late," Jesse said.

Brice tucked Shelby's hand into the crook of his arm. "You're calling first?"

"What are you talking about?" Shelby asked.

Brice grinned. "When we were in school, we usually fell for the same girl," he said. "So we made a rule that when one of us was interested in a girl and he called her first, the other three had to leave her alone."

"What did the girls have to say about that?" Shelby asked.

"We never told them," Brice said smugly.

Shelby laughed, but when she looked at Jesse, she saw his brows drawn together in a thunderous frown. He hadn't answered Brice's question about whether he was claiming first rights. Her heart jumped, and she looked away. Did she think so little of her that he didn't even want his brother to be interested? Brian was frowning as well, and the tension in the room increased a notch.

Then Mason laughed. "Just like old times with the boys squabbling over women," he said. He took Shelby's hand away from Brice. "I think your brother saw her first," he said.

Shelby nearly laughed aloud at the shock on Brice's face at his father's action. Protest and rebellion raced over his face, and he opened his mouth, but before he could speak Jesse stepped forward.

"Leave it, baby brother. I saw her first," he said. "Now how about some supper?"

The surprise on Brice's face was nothing compared to the shock that raced through Shelby. Jesse had been as aloof as she was during the past few days. What exactly did he mean by hinting he was interested in Shelby? Was it merely a ploy to deter Brice? The way Jesse's jaw muscles were set seemed to indicate some kind of emotion, but she was afraid to read anything into it.

His warm fingers around hers sent shock waves through her. She wasn't sure what to say, but luckily, Mason led the way to a table.

"Sit down, and we'll bring out your food." He held the chair for Heather, and Jesse pulled one out for Shelby, then one for Twila.

Jesse slid into the chair on Shelby's right and reclaimed her hand. She wanted to jerk it away, but he shot her a warning glance, and she left it where it was. She didn't understand, but she could grill him for an explanation when they were alone.

All through the meal, he acted very proprietary. Twila and Heather exchanged amused glances, but Shelby was mystified by it all. Her temper began to rise as Jesse hovered over her and kept his arm around the back of her chair.

Jesse's brothers flirted with her in spite of their brother's claim of ownership, and Shelby was exhausted and confused by the time the evening was over.

"Your rooms are ready," Mason said when he saw Shelby yawn.

"I'll show Shelby where her room is," Brice put in.

"I'm going that way myself," Jesse said. "Good night, all. See you in the morning." He stood, and Shelby had no choice but to stand and follow him from the dining room.

Just wait until she got him alone. He had some explaining to do.

eight

Shelby looked altogether too attractive when she was angry. Jesse fought to keep the grin from his face. He knew he'd been out of line over dinner, but this was the way it had to be. Brice would have her heart for toast. He slanted another glance at her. Her head held high, she marched down the hall at his side. Her green eyes flashed, and frenetic spots of color darkened her high cheekbones. The fists at her sides were clenched as though she'd like to punch someone, probably Jesse. Scarlet was nestled in her jacket with just the topknot of fur showing.

He liked the way she walked. Her long stride nearly matched his own, though the way she swayed was all woman. As quickly as it had come, his mirth vanished. They might have had something between them, but he had killed it by hiding the full truth. Regret twisted the corner of his mouth. There was no going back, no fixing it. She would never look up at him with that warm glow in her eyes again.

He stopped outside the best guest room. "Here we are. I'm right across the hall if you need anything."

She crossed her arms and glared at him. "What I need is an explanation. You've ignored me for the past several days then put on the charm when your family is around. Is this another of your schemes? I won't be party to it."

"Tell me what you really think of me, Shelby; don't pull any punches," he said in an ironic tone. "Do you honestly think I would do anything to hurt my family? I was trying to make sure you weren't hurt by Brice. He falls for a pretty face every week, then moves on to the next one like a bee following the flowers."

"That's a rotten thing to say about your own brother!" The green fire in her eyes threatened to burn him.

She held out her hand for her room key, but Jesse ignored her and opened the door for her himself. "I love Brice, but he's the baby of the family and is used to having what he wants. I just wanted to make sure you weren't on the menu for dessert. Unfortunately, he never wants anything for long."

Her color heightened, and she stalked into her room. She would have slammed the door in his face, but he pressed in behind her. Glancing around, he suppressed a sigh. The room was shabbier than he remembered. If this was their best room, it was no wonder the tourists weren't battering down their door to stay here.

She must have seen the discouragement on his face, for her anger faded. "What's wrong?"

He gestured around the room. "This. Would *you* want to stay here if you were on vacation?"

Shelby glanced around the room. Jesse tried to see it through her eyes. The worn and shabby bedspread lay dispiritedly on a mattress with obvious sags. The walls were blotchy with fading paint, and the curtains seemed almost devoid of color. Stains darkened the ragged carpet.

"Pretty bad, huh?" he asked. He thrust his hands into his pockets. "It's the only job my dad has ever known. Amigos was started by my grandparents in 1950. Losing it would kill my dad."

Shelby's face softened. "That still doesn't excuse not telling me the whole story," she said. Though her words were harsh, her tone was gentle.

"I've told you I'm sorry," Jesse said. He turned to go back to the hall. "The race starts in two days. You'd better get some rest."

Shelby nodded and shut the door behind him.

Jesse whistled as he walked back to the wing that housed his family. His father was reading by the fireplace. He put his book down when he saw Jesse.

Jesse dropped into the chair beside him. "How's business, Pop?"

Mason sighed and removed his reading glasses. "Slow, but it will pick up."

That's what he had been saying for two years, and every week the outlook seemed more bleak. Jesse held his tongue, though. His dad didn't need more encouragement.

"Your young lady get settled?"

"She's not my young lady," Jesse said.

"That's not what you told your brothers."

"Yeah, well, I didn't want Brice to get any ideas. I don't want Shelby to get hurt."

"Uh-huh," Mason said.

"What's that supposed to mean?"

"Just that for someone who says he has no interest in Shelby, you seem mighty concerned."

"She doesn't need another Titus giving her grief," Jesse said. "I'm not proud of how I treated her, Pop."

"She found out about the will." His father's voice was resigned.

"Yep. Now she thinks I can't be trusted. But at least she

didn't back out, which is what Palmer wanted."

"I hate to take your money, Son. Even if you win the race, maybe I should just let the old place go. Retire and take it easy."

"We're not losing it," Jesse said firmly. He couldn't imagine his dad not puttering around the grounds. And what would his brothers do? None of them knew anything but sailing and running a resort. He supposed they could all find jobs at other resorts, but they would be scattered instead of working together at their own place. He couldn't let it happen.

Mason sighed again. "Tell me again about the race. Do you think you really have a chance?"

"The *Jocelyn* is a good boat. But the crew is what makes the difference. And we're the crew, Dad. We've been training for this for years. I want this win more than any of the other captains do. My only concern is that we only get one tank of gas, so we have to sail most of the way and save that bit of fuel for becalmed days only. Pray that we don't hit any storms that force us to use more of our fuel. The first ship to round Cape Horn and dock at Falkland Island wins two hundred thousand dollars. And I also win two hundred thousand dollars from West's estate."

"And if Shelby hangs in there all the way, you get another hundred thousand from her uncle's estate. Enough to pay the bank loan." His father's voice held deep satisfaction.

"Yes." Jesse didn't like to think about that. He wanted her to finish so that she conquered her fear without thinking about what he gained. He didn't want to gain anything from Shelby's efforts. But it was too late to regret his actions now.

His father patted his shoulder. "You're a good boy, Jesse.

Just remember, you could have discouraged her from coming and have taken her entire estate. That shows your integrity." He rose and went toward the hall. "I think I'll turn in. Tomorrow you can scope out the competition."

Some integrity. If he had thought of his integrity, he would have told Shelby the full truth and not hidden it from her. Jesse got to his feet. "I'm heading to bed myself." But later, as he went to his own room and shut the door and turned out the light, he lay awake a long time listening to the waves crash on the beach. His heart ached, and he wasn't quite sure why.

The birds chirping outside her window awakened Shelby. She lay on the lumpy mattress a few minutes listening to the sweet music. Soon there would be no birds chirping, only the restless sound of the waves and wind. But the thought brought excitement as well as terror. She was stronger now, more ready to face that fearsome sea.

Swinging her legs out of bed, she nearly tripped. Scarlet yelped. "Sorry, Sweetie." She picked up her dog and petted her a moment, then put her down and went to the window. Her last day of land. What did she want to do? The small town beckoned, and she quickly dressed. She would take Scarlet out to potty, then see if Twila wanted to explore with her.

But Twila had already gone out with Heather by the time Shelby found her way to the kitchen. In fact, no one was left in the place except for Mason. He gave her directions, and she set out on her own.

Ensenado was a typical small Mexican town with vendors hawking their wares on the streets. They immediately recognized her as an American, and shouted their offers even after she shook her head and moved on. She bought some acetaminophen and aspirin, as well as cold remedies and other first aid supplies. At one shop she found a cute leather bag to keep it all in.

The sun was high overhead when she started back to the resort. Her stomach rumbled, and she realized she'd had nothing to eat all day. The tantalizing aroma of enchiladas wafted out the door of a small café, and she found a small table in the corner. Several curious glances came her way, but she merely smiled and nodded. Her Spanish was nonexistent, but she managed to order a chicken enchilada and soda. No ice, though, or she'd be paying with a stomach complaint.

Enjoying the different atmosphere, she lingered over her meal. It was nearly an hour later when she paid for her food then gathered up her bags. She squinted at the bright sunshine and nearly ran a male figure down.

"Sorry," she said.

Brian smiled down at her, but it seemed forced. Maybe he was as uncomfortable in her presence as she was in his.

"You're alone?" he asked.

She nodded. "What are you doing here?"

"Everything seemed shipshape so Jesse sent us off to enjoy ourselves for the afternoon. I was looking for you and stopped by the resort, if you can call it that."

The contempt in his voice irritated her. "They do the best they can, I expect."

"They would be better off to raze it and build new." He fell into step beside her.

"Why were you looking for me?" She wished he would

leave her alone. His attentions were beginning to get on her nerves.

"I thought I might show you the town. I've been here several times, and there are some great places to buy jewelry—but it's not the best place for a lady to be alone."

Her interest stirred in spite of her dislike for her companion. "I'm looking for something for my mother's birthday, but I didn't see anything I liked." His smile made her uneasy, but she shrugged away her trepidation.

"Follow me." He led her down narrow dirt streets with the odors of onions wafting out open doorways and past stuccoed shops with fly-speckled windows. Stopping at a modest building, he opened the door. "The prices are great and so is the selection. You should find something for your mother here."

She entered first. It didn't look like a shop, but more like a home. Wrinkling her nose at the smell of cat urine, she turned to leave, but Brian shut the door and leaned against it.

"I don't think I'm interested. Let's go back to the hotel."

His smile became mocking. "I'm not ready to leave yet."

Her unease deepened, and she moved closer to the door and put her hand on the doorknob. Brian made no move to step away and let her pass. "Please get out of my way. I'm leaving."

"I don't think so," Brian said. "I know you don't really want to go on that voyage. I've seen the fear in your eyes. We can have some fun together here in Ensenado then travel back to San Francisco together." He snapped his fingers, and a man came through the doorway.

"Enrico, would you see that our guest is comfortable? I need to let Jesse know we won't be traveling on with him."

Enrico was short and stocky with lank black hair that hung in greasy locks down his head. When he smiled, Shelby saw that most of his teeth were missing. She backed away from him, then whirled to flee. His large hands grabbed her. Thrashing to escape, she started to scream and Enrico stuffed her mouth with a filthy rag. Producing a rope from his pocket, he tied her hands behind her back and marched her to the back room.

The room was darkened by dirty curtains. He tossed her to the couch and secured the other end of the rope to the back leg of the couch. Brian followed them into the room.

"I suppose you're wondering what this is all about?" He smiled when she nodded fiercely. "Simple. Palmer is paying me very well to make sure you don't complete that voyage. It's just a little insurance against the remote possibility that Palmer might lose the race. If you fail to go around the Horn on *Jocelyn*, the loser of the race gets your inheritance."

He grinned, and Shelby felt sick.

"I'll just go back to the hotel and tell Jesse you've changed your mind. We've fallen in love and want to be together." He leaned over her and touched a strand of hair. "But don't worry. My tastes run more to small blondes, not red-haired Amazons."

She could be thankful for that. Palmer was behind this? Tears of frustration and anger stung her eyes. She had to get out of here. Working her tongue against the gag, she tried to force it out of her mouth, but it was too big. *Help me, Lord.* She took a deep, calming breath. Biting back her panic, she reminded herself she wasn't alone. She had to cling to her trust in God.

Brian patted her on the head, and she jerked away. He laughed. "I'll be back later. I suppose we can take the gag out. But Enrico will put it back if you make a peep."

The relief of getting the gag out of her mouth was overwhelming. Brian closed the door behind him and left her with Enrico. The minutes, then the hours, ticked by. Enrico watched her like a cat playing with a mouse. Working her hands against the rope, her bonds began to loosen slightly, but not enough to free herself.

Dusk fell, and Enrico flicked on the light, a pale gleam that knocked back the gloom only slightly. Enrico's grin sickened her, and her fear battled with her faltering hope. The *Jocelyn* left at six in the morning. She had to find a way to slip through this loop Palmer had fashioned.

She shifted uncomfortably. "Enrico, I need to use the bathroom."

"No comprende, señorita." Enrico shrugged his shoulders.

Her shoulders slumped. So much for that idea.

The door opened, and Brian entered. "Well, Jesse wasn't happy about it, but he had no choice but to accept it. For awhile, I thought I might have to make you call him."

"I wouldn't do it," Shelby said defiantly. "Now unfasten this rope. I need to use the bathroom."

Brian's smirk faltered. He looked uncertain, then shrugged. "Don't try anything funny." Fumbling with the rope, he untied her and jerked her to her feet. "Enrico and I will be right outside the door."

Shelby jerked out of his grasp and stalked to the bathroom. Locking the door behind her, she quickly looked around. There was one small window, but it wasn't big enough for someone her size to squeeze out of. Her heart sank. The sparsely appointed bathroom held no possible weapon.

She just had to talk Brian out of tying her up again. Flushing the toilet, she washed her hands and reluctantly opened the door. Enrico grabbed her arm and propelled her toward the couch. She jerked her arm out of his grasp.

"Don't tie me up again, okay, Brian? My arms are numb, and I'm hungry." She gave him her most winning smile.

Brian hesitated, then jerked his head at Enrico and spoke in Spanish. Enrico scowled and stomped from the room. Brian plopped on the couch. "Might as well take a load off, Sugar. Enrico won't be back for an hour or so, knowing him."

Shelby had to get away before Enrico got back. She stood a better chance of handling Brian than she did both men together. "I'm thirsty, Brian. Do you want something?"

Surprise flickered across his face, then he nodded. "The fridge is probably empty, but you can see what he's got. Just don't try anything funny."

There was nothing funny about the situation. She went through the door he indicated. There was no exit from the kitchen, and she cast around desperately for a weapon. That was one good thing about being larger than the average woman. She was also larger than many men, Brian included. Turning on the water to mask the noise, she slid open a drawer. Her gaze fastened on the knife in the drawer. It was small, but it would have to do. Shelby grasped it and slid it up her sleeve, then opened the refrigerator and took out the two lukewarm Cokes on the top shelf.

The murmur of voices stopped her. Her heart sank. Enrico was back. Her bid for escape would have to wait.

The evening dragged by. At ten Brian showed her to her room and locked her in. The only window was tiny like the one in the bathroom. Shelby paced the room. Once they went to bed, maybe she could use the knife to pick the lock on the door. Sitting gingerly on the filthy bed, she prepared to wait it out.

Her eyelids grew heavy, but she fought the drowsiness. She sank to her knees and prayed for strength and help. Shelby had never been in such a precarious situation, but in spite of her fear, she felt an overpowering sense of God's protection. Whatever happened, He was in control.

The sleepiness was almost overwhelming. She would just lay her head against the side of the bed a moment. Her eyes closed and she slept. Awakening with a start, she jerked her head up. Dread clogged her throat. How long had she slept? She may have already missed her chance.

Her gaze locked on her illuminated watch. Five o'clock. She had only an hour to escape and get to the boat. Stiffly, she got to her feet and stretched the kinks out. The floor had been hard and cold. Sidling to the door, she peered through the keyhole. It was dark and silent in the room beyond. Hope surged. She tried the door. Still locked.

Carefully, she inserted the knife blade into the keyhole. For several long minutes she poked and prodded with the knife. This wasn't going to work. Despair gripped her throat, but she persisted. Then, with a soft click, the lock released.

Shelby let her breath out with a whoosh. Noiselessly, she turned the doorknob and opened the door. The room was totally dark, but she could hear hoarse snoring from the direction of the couch. Creeping along with her hand gliding on the wall, she made her way toward the door. Her progress seemed perilously slow. She felt along with her feet, and finally she was at the doorway to the outer room.

The snore behind her paused, and her mouth went dry. The snoring resumed, and her shoulders relaxed. Inching forward again, she made her way to the door. Her hand went to the doorknob. It was locked. Hunching her shoulders, she felt for the lock. There it was. She slid it back, and it made a grinding noise. Pausing, she listened for sound from the other room, but all she heard was the snoring. She eased the door open.

The cool air cleared her head. She looked at the small knife in her hand. At the time she found it, it had seemed very inadequate. But God had known what she needed. He wouldn't let her down now. Rushing through the quiet and deserted streets, her breath whistled through her teeth. She would make it to the boat. She had to make it.

nine

Jesse paced the hall. This felt all wrong. He didn't believe Brian, but the man had given him no reason to disbelieve him, either. He had given him a note from Shelby, though he'd never seen her handwriting. The note had been very clear, but the situation still smelled bad to Jesse. Shelby wasn't one to run from a fight. She would be more likely to tell him face to face than to hare off with a lightweight like Brian, with only a cowardly note to explain her actions.

He'd cruised through the town looking for her until midnight, but there had been no sign of her tall figure. Tossing and turning, he'd finally gotten up again at three this morning but was no closer to a decision about what to do.

He paused outside the door to her room. A noise caught his attention. Someone was inside that room. His throat tightened, and he put his ear to the door. There it was again. The soft sound of movement. Jesse turned the doorknob and eased the door open a crack. Reaching inside, he flicked the light then pushed the door all the way open.

There was a yelp, then a small ball of fur hurled itself at him. Whimpering, Scarlet jumped against his leg. He caught the odor of dog urine, and the little dog whimpered in shame again. Picking her up, he patted her head. "It's okay, Scarlet, it's not your fault."

Now he knew there was something wrong. Shelby would never leave Scarlet behind. Never. With the dog still in his arms, he bounded down the hall and pounded on his dad's door.

It was several minutes before his father came to the door. "Jesse? What's wrong?" Rubbing his eyes, his scalp shone through the bald spot he tried to cover with hair from the side.

"Look." Jesse held up Scarlet. "Shelby would never leave her dog. She's Shelby's baby. This proves she only intended to be gone a short time."

Mason shrugged and yawned. "Women are fickle creatures, especially when they're in love."

"No, Dad. I know Shelby well enough to know this just isn't like her." He turned and went to the doors of the other crew members. One by one, he awakened them and explained the situation.

Twila turned and began to gather her clothes. "I'm findin' that child. I had a feelin' this wasn't right, but there's no doubt now, boss man."

"You should be down at the boat by now," Mason said. "What about the race?"

Andy and Heather stared at Jesse. Twila's steps paused as she started toward the bathroom to get dressed.

"How can you even ask? There will be other races." A ball of dread had congealed in Jesse's stomach, and the race seemed very unimportant at this moment.

Twila nodded. "And that child wouldn't go off and leave one of us. I never trusted that Brian. I don't think he knew as much about sailin' as he said he did."

Jesse fell silent for a moment. "He came with good references."

"Letters can be forged. Looks like he forged one from

Shelby yesterday," Andy put in.

"Well, you all can jaw here in the hall all you want. I'm gettin' dressed and goin' after Shelby." Her clothes in her arms, Twila continued on her way to the bathroom.

"Andy, you take the girls and head to town. I'm going to check the dock area." Jesse dropped Scarlet to the floor. "Dad, see that Scarlet gets something to eat, would you? Then get the boys up and send them out looking, too."

"Who could sleep with all this commotion?" Brice's sandy hair stood on end, and he leaned against the door jamb.

"We now think Shelby has been kidnapped," Jesse told him. "I'm going out to look."

Brice straightened up. "Hold on a minute and I'll go with you."

"Get our stuff onboard the boat, then meet me at the dock. I'm heading there now." Jesse didn't wait for an answer but headed down the hall. He should feel worse about the race, but he couldn't even think of it. The worry about Shelby crowded out every other concern.

He cared about her. The knowledge took him by surprise. He'd only known her less than two weeks, but she'd crept into his heart in spite of his trying to keep her at arm's length. His stride lengthened. He had to find her. And God knew where she was. He prayed that He would guide him to the right place.

The town was beginning to awaken as he strode through the streets. Where could he look first? He should have followed Brian yesterday, but he'd been so astonished by Brian's assertion that Shelby was leaving with him, he hadn't thought of it until the man was out of sight.

He stopped fishermen and described Shelby. One by one they all shook their heads and continued on their way. Glancing at his watch, he saw it was already five-thirty. The race would be starting in half an hour. Even if they got onboard right now, they would likely be the last ones to leave the harbor. But he couldn't worry about that. Thrusting his hands into his pockets, he walked back toward town. Maybe the rest of the crew had better luck.

"Jesse!"

His heart jumped at the familiar voice. Squinting in the lightening gloom, he saw Shelby's tall figure running down the middle of the street. Behind her were Andy, Heather, and Twila. Joy squeezed his heart.

As she reached his side, he grabbed her and swept her into an embrace. "Thank the good Lord you're safe." After a moment's hesitation, Shelby clung to him. He released her reluctantly. "Let's go; we might just make the race. Brice has our stuff stored by now. You can explain onboard."

The light in Shelby's eyes faded, but she fell into step with him and loped along at his side with long strides. He wished he could take time to reassure her that he cared what happened to her, but there would be time for that on the long voyage ahead. Over six months at sea would give him plenty of time for explanations.

His brothers were all onboard when they got to the boat. The other competitors had their sails readied, and Jesse's heart sank at the monumental task ahead of them.

"I'm going with you!" Brice dropped his backpack into the hold and whirled to give them a hand boarding. "You're one man short." He took Scarlet from his jacket and dropped her down the hold, too.

Jesse wasted no time in thanks. "Hoist the mainsail, and get ready to loose the mooring lines," he ordered. "We'll take a starboard tack."

The crew flew into action while his brothers and father jumped off the boat and went to walk the *Jocelyn* away from the dock.

"I'll check the bilge," Shelby said.

The men ran to the rigging while Heather and Twila prepared the halyards. Within minutes they were ready. The shot to start the race came before they were quite ready.

Shelby came up from the bilge. "I pumped out what water there was, but it wasn't much."

"We're going to be last out of the harbor," Heather said.

"Won't matter," Jesse said. "Where we finish is all that matters."

His reassuring words didn't erase the expression of guilt and shame on Shelby's face. He saw the sheen of tears in her eyes and wished there was time to hold her and tell her it didn't matter. But if they were going to make a start in this race at all, they had to concentrate and get going.

The sails were hoisted, and the women coiled the lines.

"Dad, release the mooring line," Jesse said.

His father obeyed. The sails were plump, and the boat heeled away from the wind.

"Trim the headsail," Jesse shouted.

The boat righted slightly then began to move toward the other boats. The crew cheered.

"We made it!" An overwhelming relief swept over Jesse.

"God speed, Jesse!" Kane called across the water.

"We'll be praying!" Aaron added.

Mason gave them a thumbs-up. A lump in his throat,

Jesse waved back. They were all depending on him. And they were all in God's hands.

❦

Shelby felt ill and trembly inside. After the trauma of the past twelve hours, tears hovered near the surface. It was reaction, she knew, but she hated to be the cause of their late start. She pushed the nagging thoughts away and glanced at her watch. The morning had flown by as they all did their best to make up for their late start. Eleven-thirty. Time to prepare lunch.

There was a stiff wind to their backs, but they were still behind the rest of the boats. Jesse stalked the deck shouting orders and fine-tuning the position of the sails. He hadn't said more than two words to Shelby. She couldn't decide if it was distraction or recrimination that she sensed in his attitude.

Shelby bit her lip and went below. Taking out her recipe box, she found the menu she'd planned for today. Spam sandwiches and macaroni salad for lunch. The pot roast and potatoes for supper needed to be put into the oven, too. She busied herself with the meal preparations, then called the crew to eat at twelve-thirty.

"Where's Jesse?" she asked when he didn't come down the ladder.

"At the helm. He said he'd eat later, when one of us could spell him," Andy said. "I tried to get him to let me take a turn now. I know he didn't get any breakfast."

"None of us did," Twila reminded him.

Their sacrifice on her behalf touched Shelby. They really cared about her. She wished she'd fixed a bigger lunch to make up for it. "I'll take him up a plate," she said.

"You eat," Brice urged. "My brother is a big boy. I bet you haven't eaten, either."

"I'm not really hungry." Her stomach roiled at the thought of food. She wouldn't be able to rest until she knew what Jesse was thinking. He needed to be told that she would never abandon the voyage by choice.

Shelby prepared a plate with generous portions then grabbed a soda from the refrigerator. Climbing the ladder, she picked her way through the coiled lines to Jesse's side at the helm.

He glanced at her briefly before turning back to scan the horizon. "You didn't have to do that. Brice was going to take control of the helm as soon as he ate."

"I thought you might be hungry."

"I am, but I could have waited. Thanks." He took the sandwich and bit into it. "I love Spam," he said. "We eat a lot of it, so it always reminds me of the sea."

Shelby laughed. "I was afraid you would all moan at the mention of it. I can't say I'm that fond of it myself."

"You will be by the time the trip is over." He glanced her way again. "You feel up to telling me what happened?"

"That's why I came up here," she admitted.

Jesse nodded. "I'm sorry I wasn't more welcoming when we found you, but there was no time."

"You aren't mad at me? You may lose the race because of me."

He shook his head. "There's a lot of water between here and the Cape. Many of the boats ahead of us won't make it. Besides, we are actually in the race. For a while this morning, I wasn't too sure we would be."

Shock rippled through her. "You weren't going to go?"

His eyes widened as he looked at her again. "We wouldn't leave you."

"How did you know I didn't want to be left?" That question had been bothering her.

"Simple." He grinned. "Scarlet."

A dawning comprehension came over her. "Of course! You knew I wouldn't leave her behind."

"Exactly. But even before that, I didn't believe Brian. You would have enjoyed telling me to take a hike too much to let Brian do it."

Shelby laughed. "I'm always polite."

"You're always blunt," Jesse corrected, but he softened his words with a smile. "But I still don't know why Brian would do this."

"He's working for Palmer."

"Palmer!" Jesse fell silent a moment. "I wonder if Brian had anything to do with wrecking my boat?"

"I wouldn't be surprised. Palmer wants me to fail my uncle's requirement of sailing around the Horn so he can inherit everything if he loses the race." She sighed. "I still find it hard to believe. Uncle Lloyd always thought so highly of Palmer. And he seemed the perfect gentleman."

"You just don't know him that well," Jesse pointed out. "He's known at the yacht club as tenacious enough to do anything, even cheat, to win. And I've heard he's been in some financial trouble."

Shelby felt dizzy with relief at his calm acceptance of her explanation. He wasn't angry with her. She didn't want to examine too closely just why it mattered.

"Now tell me what happened and how you got away," Jesse commanded.

His frown deepened as she explained the events of the previous day. "I wish there had been time to press charges against him."

"We've got Brice now. He'll be a better crewman than Brian. Seems a fair trade," Shelby told him.

Instead of that statement lightening his frown, it deepened. "Remember what I said and stay away from Brice," Jesse said. "He's not for you."

Where had the camaraderie of the last few minutes gone? Here he was dictating to her again. He might be Brice's big brother, but he had no right to tell either one of them what to do.

He must have seen her stiffen, for he held up a placating hand. "Don't get your back up. I'm just thinking of you."

"I think my love life is none of your business. And neither is Brice's." She took the empty plate from his hand and stalked back toward the galley. One minute she thought friendship might be possible with Jesse, and the next minute he made her mad enough to spit. And men thought women were unpredictable!

Over the next few days, Shelby kept her distance from Jesse. But she found it harder to keep away from Brice. In the confines of a fifty-two-foot boat, there was really no way to avoid someone who was determined to be underfoot. And Brice was determined. Shelby couldn't deny that she felt flattered by his attention. He was a handsome man, and the look in his eyes told her he found her attractive. It was balm for the bruised feelings she still nursed from Jesse.

Shelby stood staring out at the white-capped waves. She hadn't been aware that the voyage would become so boring. The months ahead stretched out, and she wondered what she could do to keep boredom away. She sighed and glanced at her watch. It was almost time to prepare supper, and as she went below, an idea struck her. Her eyes widened, and her heart pounded with excitement. She'd always wanted to do something with cooking. What about a cookbook of her own? One for would-be sailors who took advantage of the experience she was gaining aboard ship with canned and frozen food. She could title it *A Ship's Cook Cooks*. That was a catchy title.

Her hands trembled as she prepared the meal. She had a hundred Spam recipes. And all kinds of casseroles that used tinned food. It was almost as if the idea was a clear gift from God. She just knew it would be successful.

As soon as the supper dishes were washed and cleared away, she excused herself and went to her cabin. Luckily, she'd brought several tablets of paper in her sea chest. Rummaging in the chest, she found them and laid them to one side. One of these days she would go through the contents of the chest and get to know her uncle a little better. He had all kinds of log books and navigational tools in there.

When she went back to the galley to write down all the ingredients she'd brought to cook, she found Jesse seated at the kitchen table.

His glance sharpened when he saw her. "You feeling okay? Your cheeks are red."

"I'm fine," she said. She knew she should keep the plan to herself, but she was too excited. "I'm going to write a book!"

She wondered if he would laugh, but he merely tipped his chair back and regarded her with those dark eyes that she found so disconcerting.

"What about?"

Because he seemed so genuinely interested, she found herself telling him. "I've thought about opening my own business where I go into homes and prepare and freeze meals ahead for busy working women. Since cooking is what I love, I'm going to write a cookbook for people on voyages like this one."

Jesse nodded slowly. "Sounds like an idea that will sell. When we get back, I'll introduce you to my cousin, Roger Merger. He's an acquisitions editor for a big publishing house in New York."

"You'd do that for me?"

Jesse set his chair back. "Why does that surprise you? I like you, Shelby. I think you have great talent." He grinned. "I'd even endorse your cooking."

He liked her. Heat scorched her cheeks, and she felt a little sick. She was very afraid she more than liked Jesse Titus. She forced a smile. "Thanks, Jesse. I'd appreciate that."

The silence between them drew out, then Jesse got to his feet. "I'd better check on how we're tacking before bed." He started toward the ladder, then stopped in front of her.

Shelby saw his gaze linger on her lips, and for one heart-stopping moment, she thought he might kiss her. She held her breath, but then the warmth of his eyes cooled. "You're on for watch from one to three this morning. Think you can handle it?"

She nodded. "I can work on my recipes to stay awake."

He chuckled. "I'll wake you when it's your turn."

She watched his broad shoulders navigate the close confines of the hold. This voyage was maybe going to be more of a mistake than she had realized. Daily, she was more and more drawn to him. He was firm yet kind with the crew, and knowledgeable, but he didn't ridicule when she had a question. She didn't want to feel this way. It wasn't safe for her heart.

ten

Shelby's heart was still overflowing with thankfulness at the direction God had given her. After feeling adrift without an oar for the past several years, she was eager to walk through the door God had opened in her heart. But she had to get some sleep. There would be plenty of time to work on the book, and one o'clock would come sooner than she would like.

She read her Bible then crawled into bed. Twila was already asleep. She'd come down with a bad cold and had barely managed to stay awake through supper.

In spite of her excitement, her eyes were heavy, and she fell asleep almost as soon as her head hit the pillow. She was dreaming that her mother was knocking at the door of their new home, when she realized the knocking was real. Forcing her eyes open, she fumbled for the lamp.

"Coming," she called softly. She glanced to where Twila lay humped beneath her quilt, but the other woman didn't stir. She grabbed her notebook and a pen, then flipped off the light and stepped outside the cabin.

Jesse's eyes were shadowed with fatigue, but he smiled down at her. "You ready for this?"

She wasn't, but she nodded.

"Just keep an eye out for the way the boat is tacking. It should stay on a steady course without too much work from you." He yawned.

"You need to get to bed. I'll be fine."

He nodded. "See you in the morning."

She smiled and headed to the navigation cabin. The stars glittered in the onyx sky like diamonds on a black velvet dress. The creak of the mast and the flap of the sails gave Shelby a mournful feeling, as though she were all alone in the boat. She felt very small and vulnerable. The boat was just a small bobber in the vast ocean with the blackness pressing in on her. Blackness below the water, blackness above. If she slipped overboard, the boat would sail on without her, and no one would ever find her in that dark void.

Her fingers trembled as she gripped her pen and focused the light on her notebook. She would write some recipe ideas to try on the crew. That would get her mind off the way the black vastness pressed in on her from every side. Would she ever be free from this fear?

Chewing on the end of the pen, she began to write, glancing now and then at the sails and the compass. Everything was running perfectly, but the inner trembling didn't go away. She tossed her pen down and stood to stretch. Daylight was still hours away. She would be happy if she could stay below and never have to be on the deck, especially at night.

A sound came from behind her. She froze, imagining the sinuous arm of a giant squid feeling its way along the deck. Her throat closed with terror, and she opened her mouth to scream when she saw Jesse's familiar broad shoulders. She let out her breath in a whoosh.

"Jesse," she croaked.

His gaze went to her face. "You're white as an albino seal. What's wrong?"

"Don't you know better than to sneak up on a person?" She swallowed the fear that had threatened to choke her.

He held out his palms in a placating manner. "I was worried about you."

"Well, you caused me to lose five years of my life."

He chuckled. "Did you think an ax murderer had sneaked aboard?"

"A giant squid is much more terrifying to me," she said with a chagrined smile.

His grin widened, and he laughed aloud. "You've been watching too much Discovery Channel." He shut the cabin door behind him and dropped into the seat beside her. "You want some company for awhile?"

"You should be sleeping. You have dark circles under your eyes. I'll be fine now that you've assured me there's no giant squid looking to grab me."

He chuckled again. "I'm sure you'd make a tasty morsel, but the squid likes fish, not females."

He was way too close for Shelby's peace of mind. The musky scent of his cologne wafted toward her, and she wondered what he would do if she leaned over and ran her fingers through his crisp curls. Probably overturn his chair in his haste to get away. She just didn't know what he thought or felt about her. The strain of the earlier deception had never gone away. He had told her the truth since then—she was sure of that—but she didn't know how to read any signals of interest from him anymore. How much of the admiration she sometimes caught in his eyes was merely an attempt to keep her away from Brice?

He glanced at his watch. "Time for bed for you. Brice should be here any minute."

"I'll go wake him." Shelby rose and started toward the door, but Jesse stopped her with a hand on her arm.

"He has an alarm. He'll be along shortly."

The wind gusted, and the boat lurched. Shelby lost her balance and landed in Jesse's lap. His arms automatically steadied her, and the terror the wind had caused leached out of Shelby. The haven of his arms felt like coming home.

He tucked a stray hair behind her ear and ran his thumb over her cheek. Her insides felt shivery, and she caught her breath. Whatever she was feeling, he felt it, too, for his eyes darkened, and his gaze dropped to her lips.

Shelby's joking words died in her throat. The trembling in her limbs increased. Then Jesse bent his head, and his lips claimed hers. The scent of his skin and the taste of his lips assaulted her with sensation, but with more than mere physical attraction. Her arms crept around his neck, and she clung to him while the boat pitched once again.

Jesse raised his head and smiled crookedly, but before he could say anything, Shelby heard Brice's familiar whistle. Jesse's arms dropped, and she hastily got to her feet. She was sure her face mirrored the regret she saw on Jesse's.

"My turn at the helm, Darlin'," he said. His gaze went from her hot cheeks to Jesse's face. He frowned but didn't say anything else.

Shelby breathed a sigh of relief as she hurried from the navigation cabin. She would do well to stay away from Jesse. At least until this trip was over and she was sure what his true motives were.

Shelby spent the next few weeks trying new recipes, working on her book, and avoiding Jesse Titus. Brice was harder to avoid, as he actively pursued her. He ignored

Jesse's warning glances and Shelby's pointed attempts to excuse herself when he found her alone. Part of her wished his brother was that persistent, while the rational part whispered that it was all for the best.

A few days north of the equator, Jesse asked her to check the bilge. She hated that duty. The sight of water seeping into the hold frightened her and brought images of massive waves crashing through the hull and taking the boat to the bottom of the ocean.

Always before there had been only an inch or two to be pumped out, but today the bilge held nearly a foot of water. Shelby's eyes widened, and she backed away. Whirling, she shouted for Jesse.

"Whoa, slow down; it's all right." Jesse caught her by the shoulders.

"The bilge," she panted. "There's too much water in the bilge. Are we sinking?"

He draped an arm around her shoulders and walked her back toward the bilge. "I'm sure it's fine," he told her. "Let's have a look-see."

Opening the hatch, he peered into the bilge. The silence stretched on too long for Shelby. She caught at his arm. "Are–are we sinking?"

"Well, it's not good," Jesse said finally. "I'm probably going to have go under the boat and see if I can figure out where it's getting in. Otherwise, it will slow us down too much." He must have seen her eyes widen with terror, for he hugged her to his chest.

Shelby wanted to burrow her head against him and beg him not to go into that bottomless ocean, but she gathered her courage. "How can I help?"

Surprise lifted his eyebrows. "I'm going to change clothes. Have Andy strike the sails. Then you can come back and run the bilge pump." He clapped a hand on her shoulder. "Thanks, Shelby."

His simple gesture and gentle words calmed her as nothing else could. She was beginning to feel a part of the crew—part of a family almost. The only family she'd ever had was her mother, and she'd always felt more like the adult in that relationship, with all her mother's health issues.

She told the crew what was happening, then hurried back to the forward hatch and pumped the water out. Shutting off the pump, she turned and saw Jesse preparing to go overboard. He was in swimming trunks and wore a pouch of hand tools around his waist; a line was tied about his waist as well.

A deep trembling shook her limbs. What if the line broke and the boat drifted away? And what about dangerous creatures below the waves? There was no sign of land—there hadn't been for weeks. Her heart in her mouth, she watched him give a jaunty wave to the crew and dive overboard.

"Don't look so scared, Child," Twila said. "That boy knows how to take care of himself. He'll find the leak."

Shelby gave her a wan smile and gripped the railing. Peering over the side, she sought a glimpse of Jesse's figure under the water. There was not a glimmer under the white-capped waves. A minute passed, and then another; the crew watched and waited.

Then Jesse's head broke the surface of the water, and he gave them a thumbs-up. "Found it! A bolt has worked loose. I know where it is, so I can weld it from inside." He started to swim back to the boat.

A silver flash caught Shelby's eyes. Turning to look, she saw a fin slicing through the water. She opened her mouth to scream, but nothing came out at first, then she found her voice. "Shark!" she shrieked.

The rest of the crew turned to look, but Jesse didn't pause. His muscular arms cut through the water, and he reached the ladder. Brice was leaning over the side as far as he could and grabbed his brother by the loop on the rope. He and Andy pulled Jesse to the deck while the gray shape vanished under the yacht. Tears of relief sprang to Shelby's eyes.

Gasping with exertion, Jesse bent over at the waist. He peered over the boat as the silver torpedo flashed by again. He turned and grinned at Shelby. "False alarm, Shelby, but thanks for being vigilant. It's a dolphin."

Shelby could see that now, but in spite of her relief, she still felt the sharp taste of fear. Tears sprang to her eyes, and she looked away.

Jesse stepped nearer. "Hey, what's with the tears? I still have all my body parts."

She couldn't speak. Swallowing, she tried again. "You don't have to go under again, do you?" It had been a dolphin this time, but the next time they might not be so lucky.

"You offering to go next time?"

Shelby tried to smile at his obvious joke, but to her horror, she found tears spurting instead.

"I was kidding," he said. He put an arm around her.

"You're wet and cold. You'd better change," she managed.

"I could use a snack and something to drink," he told her.

"I'll meet you in the kitchen," she said.

"I'll fix that leak if you show me where it is first," Brice said. "I'm a better welder than you are." His cheeky grin diffused the tense atmosphere, and the rest of the crew laughed.

"That's the only thing you're better at." Jesse dropped his arm from Shelby's shoulders.

"I'll get your snack," Shelby said. Her tears were still threateningly close, and she had to get away before she embarrassed herself. She was reeling from the realization that Jesse had become way too important to her. It wasn't simply physical attraction or just liking. When for one heart-stopping moment she thought she might lose him, she had realized how devastating that loss would be. She had to weed out that yearning she felt for him. He would just hurt her again.

She escaped to the galley, where Scarlet greeted her with a wag of her tail and a welcoming lick when she picked her up. Scarlet welcomed her affection. She was very afraid Jesse would not. His one goal was to save his resort. She was merely a means to an end, and she had best remember that.

She made sure there was no evidence of her strain by the time the crew came down for supper. Chicken fettuccine and fresh bread brought smiles to their faces.

"Deciding to bring Shelby along to cook was the best decision you ever made," Andy said after Jesse gave thanks.

Heather punched him in the stomach. "You're going to have to go on a diet. I think you've gained ten pounds."

Andy looked wounded. "I thought you would be happy there was more of me to love."

Heather grabbed his slight paunch and pinched it.

"Ow!" he complained.

Jesse laughed, but he had a distracted air, and Shelby

noticed that he didn't look her way throughout the entire meal. Dread clutched her. Had she betrayed her feelings by her relief at his safety? The burn of shame stung her cheeks, and she rose and went to the sink and began to run water to clean up. The humiliation would be too great to bear if he suspected she loved him.

As soon as the galley was cleaned, she excused herself and went to her cabin. Opening her Bible, she flipped to 1 Corinthians chapter 13. Verses four through eight said, "Love is patient, love is kind. It does not envy, it does not boast, is not proud. It is not rude, it is not self-seeking, it is not easily angered, it keeps no record of wrongs. Love does not delight in evil but rejoices with the truth. It always trusts, always hopes, always perseveres. Love never fails."

A pretty tall order. Was what she felt for Jesse true love? Could she treat Jesse like that even if he never returned her love? Did she want to find out, or was she too frightened of rejection to risk her heart?

Twila came in and shut the door behind her. Yawning, she gathered her nightclothes and went to the head. When she came out dressed for bed, Shelby put down her Bible and climbed into bed. "You have a watch tonight?"

"Sure do, Child. But I'm not too tired if you want to talk." Her black eyes were full of compassion.

"What about?" Shelby's heart began to pound, and her ears rang with anxiety.

"I'm not blind, Child. You love Jesse, don't you?" Twila curled on the bed beside Shelby and drew her knees to her chest.

Shelby bit her lip. Her worst fears were realized—she had betrayed herself.

"Don't worry, Child. I don't think anyone else noticed but me and maybe Heather. Men aren't too observant about matters of the heart." Twila patted her knee.

"I don't want to love him," Shelby choked out. "He thinks of me as a nuisance he had to bring along to save his resort."

"You listen to me, Child. I've known Jesse Titus since he was in diapers. He loves you, he just doesn't know it yet. Right now he's strugglin' with the burden his daddy left on his shoulders, but when this voyage is over and he knows he's saved his daddy from ruin, he'll be free to follow where his heart leads him."

"His heart won't lead him my way," Shelby said firmly.

"Why not? You're a pretty girl, and you have a big heart. Jesse needs someone like you, someone who will stand up to him and be a partner, not a doormat. He's used to living with men all his life, so he's just not sure how to woo a woman. You'll just have to show him."

Shelby laughed. "How would I know how to show him? I've never been wooed by any man. Most men are afraid of me; I'm too big and too independent."

"What's Jesse, a wimp who runs from a gal who knows her own mind?" Twila shook her head. "You mark my words, Shelby West. Jesse has his heart set on you. Once he figures that out, there'll be no stoppin' him. He's got that Titus charm like his daddy. You won't be able to resist."

She had to resist. Twila was wrong. Jesse's only goal was to win this race and save the resort. It was a fact that pained her, but it was a fact nonetheless.

eleven

The warm tropical air felt good on Jesse's bare arms. A pod of dolphins swam beside the boat, and he wished they had time to stop and frolic in the water with them. They should come to the equator today. They'd enjoyed an all day-spinnaker run so far.

He turned as Twila came toward him. "You look a little green around the gills, Twila. You have *mal de mer* today? The sea hasn't been that rough." He tried to keep the concern out of his voice. He'd noticed that she didn't seem herself this trip. And in spite of his question, she had never been prone to seasickness.

Twila smiled, but Jesse thought it looked forced. "Your girlfriend doesn't snore, if that's what you're insinuatin', Son."

A muscle in his jaw twitched. "She's not my girlfriend."

"Why don't I believe that? I've seen the way you stare at her when no one is lookin'. You're goin' to hold back so long, Brice will shut you out with her." Twila leaned against the railing, and her breathing was labored.

Jesse made a mental note to ask Heather to take a look at Twila. Sometimes it paid to have a physician's assistant aboard. Then her words penetrated, and he frowned. "Brice will hurt her if she's not careful."

"What are you goin' to do about it?" She folded her arms across her chest.

"I've warned her; that's all I can do." What did Twila expect him to do? Keep her locked in her cabin? Maybe he should have a talk with his brother.

"He's in the kitchen moonin' over her right now."

Jesse clenched his jaw. "It's none of my business. Shelby has already told me that in no uncertain terms."

Twila clicked her tongue, but Heather appeared before she could answer.

"There you are, Heather. I was about to come looking for you. Take a look at Twila, would you? She's feeling under the weather."

Heather's gaze sharpened, and she stared into Twila's pasty face. "Let's go to your cabin, Kiddo. I don't like the look of you."

Twila bit her lip, then nodded grudgingly. "I do feel a little punk. But I'm up for navigation duty right now."

"I'll work a bit longer. Send Brice up to take her place on your way down," he told Heather.

She nodded. "To bed with you, Mom." She gave Twila a gentle push and followed her down into the hold.

Minutes later, Brice came up the ladder. Jesse's jaw tightened at his brother's whistle. What was wrong with him? He loved Brice, but lately all he'd felt toward him was irritation.

"Heather said you wanted to see me." Brice folded his arms across his chest.

"I need you to take Twila's turn at the wheel. She's sick."

"No problem." Brice came closer. "What's been eating you, Jesse? You mad at me about something? You've been like a grizzly with a splinter lately."

Shame washed over Jesse. This was his brother, and he

loved him. He had to get these feelings for Shelby under control and behind him. She didn't trust him; there was no chance of a real relationship.

There it was again. Trust. His biggest personal failing. Where was his own trust in God? Since his boat had been destroyed, all he'd done was scheme and plan on how to make everything turn out the way he wanted it.

Why should Shelby trust him? He'd done nothing to earn it. From keeping the full truth from her to growling at her for spending time with Brice, he'd hardly been a source of strength for her. And what about her fear of the sea? He'd been so bent on making up his late start, he had done nothing to help her overcome her fear. She still gripped a firm hold when on deck and took her turn at the wheel with a white face.

He resolved to do better with her. His emotions mustn't be allowed to get in the way of what was best for Shelby and for the rest of the crew.

Brice raised an eyebrow at his long silence. "Okay, so don't tell me." He brushed by Jesse and began to record their heading in the log.

"Sorry, little brother." Jesse squeezed Brice's shoulder, but his brother didn't turn around.

"Yeah, well, sorry isn't good enough. I'm sick and tired of being your whipping boy. I've never seen you act like this, Jesse. It's Shelby, isn't it? Well, I'm not going to give her up. This is the first woman I've met that I could imagine spending the rest of my life with. We aren't kids anymore."

Jesse kept a rein on his temper with difficulty. "This is a real woman we're discussing. You can't go after her just because of a childish rivalry with me."

Brice slammed down the logbook. "Haven't you been listening? I think I might love Shelby."

"What about Rachel, or the one before her? Jennifer, wasn't it? You told me you loved them, too. I don't want to see Shelby hurt. She's been through enough." Jesse raked a hand through his hair. Exasperation made him raise his voice.

Brice stared at him. "You're in love with her yourself, aren't you? It's not just that you saw her first, you've actually fallen for her!" A grin replaced his scowl, then flickered and died as quickly as it was born. "Then may the best man win, Jesse, because I'm not giving her up. Shelby can make up her own mind."

Jesse refused to let his brother goad him into something he wasn't ready for. "Try to think of Shelby, Brice, not yourself."

Before Brice could answer, the sails sagged and hung limp on their masts. An eerie quiet descended. Jesse had been so used to the clang of the rings and flap of sail, he jerked to look at the sails.

Brice followed him. They stared at one another a moment.

"I'd hoped we would escape the Doldrums," Jesse said. "We're in them."

Brice nodded. "Looks like we might be here awhile. There's not a cloud in the sky."

"Guess we'd better pray for a storm." Jesse stared over the railing at the dolphins playing near the starboard side.

Shelby came up to the deck.

"What's going on?" Shelby's voice was fearful.

"We're in the Doldrums," Jesse told her.

"The Doldrums?"

"Near the equator the trade winds die, or what we have swirl in all directions so that we can't make any progress. There's no wind."

"What do we do?" The fear in Shelby's voice increased a notch.

"We have two choices. We can wait awhile and hope we get a squall to blow us out of here, or we can use the motor and some of our gas. In a near tie, the boat with the greatest amount of fuel left wins. I'm inclined to hold out for at least a day or two and hope for some wind. We're making good time, and we have a long way to go yet."

Deep, portentous steps sounded behind them. Jesse turned to see a figure with a white flowing beard and wearing a purple robe come toward him carrying a trident and bearing Andy's twinkling blue eyes.

He banged the trident on the deck. "King Neptune's court is now in session. Be seated."

Shelby's eyes widened, and Jesse suppressed a grin. He sank onto the deck, and after a moment's hesitation, Shelby sat beside him. "Brice, would you fetch Heather and see if Twila feels up to joining us?"

Brice grinned and went down the hatch. Minutes later, the other two women appeared. Jesse was relieved to see that Twila's color looked better. The rest of the crew sat on the deck in a semicircle around King Neptune.

"Let us begin," King Neptune said in a deep voice. He pointed a finger at Heather. "You, Ma'am, are accused of polluting the ocean a month ago with the contents of your stomach. You also are charged with eating everything on your plate and still staying disgustingly thin. How do you plead?"

Heather barely managed to keep her grin in check. "Guilty as charged."

King Neptune turned his gaze to Jesse. "Jesse Titus, you are charged with sleeping while off duty and with bringing your disgustingly dirty tennis shoes onboard the new boat despite the fact that you were clearly warned before the trip to get new ones. How do you plead?"

"I brought new tennis shoes, I just haven't worn them yet," Jesse said.

"Silence! Your crimes are apparent!" He stroked his long beard. "Twila Connors, you are accused of hogging the helm and also of not sharing your gum when requested. How do you plead?"

"Guilty," Twila said. Her dark eyes were sparkling, and she squeezed Shelby's hand.

"Brice Titus, you are charged with very serious crimes. This court has been informed that you hourglassed the spinnaker yesterday. You are accused of flirting with Shelby West and distracting her from her duties. How do you plead?"

"Guilty." Brice's grin widened.

"Now we come to the most grievous crimes. You, Shelby West, are accused of preparing such delicious meals that most members have gained too much weight for their clothes to fit properly. You are also charged with being reluctant to take a voyage with such delightful companions. How do you plead?"

"Not guilty," Shelby said meekly.

"Silence! Your crimes are proven by the evidence." King Neptune patted his rounded belly. He turned his gaze on Jesse. "Mr. Titus, I would ask you to administer the usual punishment."

Jesse got to his feet and bowed to the court. "Yes, King. Excuse me while I prepare the punishment." He ducked down the hatch and went to the galley. Within minutes he had concocted a mixture of kitchen scraps from lunch, heavy amounts of garlic, and some dog food for good measure. That ought to make them cringe.

He went to the hatch and called up the steps. "Oh, King Neptune, could you come here a minute?" He heard Andy admonish the prisoners to stay put and not try to escape their punishment, then he clambered down the steps, pulling off his costume as he came. Jesse took the costume and quickly donned it.

He hurried up the hatch. Once on deck, he turned and called down, "Andy Everest, you have not yet been summoned before this court."

Andy scampered up to the deck and stood before him with an abject air. "Yes, O King."

"You have been charged with coaxing Shelby into fixing too many cookies, and also with snoring and keeping the rest of the crew awake. How do you plead?"

"Guilty!" Heather said.

Jesse turned a quelling stare on her. "Silence! The prisoner must answer for himself."

"Guilty as charged, your honor." Andy bowed his head.

"Administer the punishment, Sir. I will assist you." He followed Andy down the hatch, and they laughed like two kids as they split the concoction into two pails and went back up on the deck. The rest of the crew knew what to expect, but Shelby stood wide-eyed off to one side, with Scarlet in her arms.

"I would suggest putting Scarlet down," Andy said.

Slowly, Shelby dropped her dog to the deck. Her nose wrinkled when she saw what they were carrying. "What are you going to do with that?"

"One, two, three!" Jesse muttered. In one synchronized movement, they doused the entire crew with the contents of the buckets.

"Ew, yuck, dog food," Heather complained.

Shelby's eyes were wide with shock. She stared at the men, then down at the rivulets of goop staining her T-shirt, then back at the men.

"Now you must all swim over the equator," Andy said.

Heather yelped but immediately took a running leap over the side of the boat. Andy followed with a graceful somersault. Brice cannonballed with a huge splash that left Shelby dripping with water.

Only Shelby, Twila, and Jesse remained aboard.

"One person has to be aboard at all times," Twila said. "You two go first, and I'll wait until you get back."

Shelby's eyes widened. "I–I can't," she whispered. "You know I can't." She backed away from him as though from a snake or a spider.

Jesse put out his hand and touched her. "I won't let anything happen to you, Shelby. You can wear your life jacket."

"What if there are things under the water?" The muscles in her throat moved.

"They won't hurt you. We haven't seen any sharks in weeks."

"But they could come at any time."

He had to admit that was possible. But not likely. "Just for a few minutes."

She shook her head violently, and her ponytail whipped

back and forth. Her face was white with fear. "I'm sorry. I can't."

He shrugged. "You'd better shower then. In this heat, you'll soon start to attract scavenger birds." It was a feeble joke, but he wanted to erase that expression of sheer terror from her eyes.

Shelby nodded. "H–have fun." She turned away and hurried toward the hatch.

Jesse watched her follow Twila to the helm, then he scooped up Scarlet. "Your mistress might be too scared, but I bet you'd enjoy a swim, Scarlet. You game to be my date?" The dog licked him, and he took that as a yes. "Geronimo!" he yelled as he jumped over the side. Scarlet gave an excited yip, and they were swimming in water as warm as a bath. It would be paradise if Shelby had joined him.

❦

Shelby was still trembling from the very thought of going overboard into the vast ocean. How could they do it so eagerly? She had thought she would be over this ridiculous fear by now, but if anything, it was even stronger. "Why, Lord?" she whispered. "Why can't You just take this fear away? You could do it if You just would."

She watched Twila leaning against the wheel, her breathing harsh and labored. "Are you all right?" Shelby asked her.

"Just tired," Twila said.

"You've been tired a lot lately. And you haven't been sleeping well. Why don't you let me be mom for awhile?" Shelby fished a couple of pieces of sour candy out of her pocket and handed one to Twila.

"Thanks." Twila unwrapped it and popped it into her mouth.

Shelby thought her friend's dusky skin looked almost yellow. "What's wrong, Twila? I can keep a confidence."

"I don't want the others to know until the voyage is over," she said. "And I don't want you fussin' over me, either. I was goin' to tell Heather, but King Neptune intervened." She gave a soft laugh.

"I won't say a thing." Shelby's uneasiness heightened. Twila reached out a trembling hand and sank shakily into the helmsman's seat. Shelby was shaken to see the normally calm and confident Twila in such a weak state.

"I'm dying," Twila said blandly.

Shelby's breath left her. "No," she whispered. She couldn't have heard her correctly.

"Liver cancer," Twila said as though she had just told Shelby she had a cold. "The doctors wanted to try somethin' experimental, but I refused. I want to enjoy my final days not layin' in a hospital bed somewhere. I'm hopin' it comes while I'm at sea. That would be the best way to go. Lookin' up into the heavens is like lookin' into the face of God."

"How—" Shelby broke off, unsure of how to ask. The shock was beginning to wear off, and pain at the impending loss of her friend was gnawing at her. She'd never had a best friend before, and Twila had taught her what a true friend was.

"How long? The doctors said maybe three months. If that's true, God will likely receive me right from this boat." She said the words with satisfaction.

"You don't seem to be afraid." Shelby wondered how she

would feel if she was the one facing death. Probably terrified. That's what scared her about the ocean. It was like immersing herself in the unknown. Even knowing God was at the other end of life, it was hard to imagine. She liked being in control, and death took all that pretense away.

Twila gave her a slight smile. "My mama and daddy are waitin' for me along with Jesus. What's to be afraid of, Child?"

When she put it like that, it didn't seem so terrifying. "What can I do to help you?"

"I have my pain medication, and I'll tell Heather as soon as I can. Nothin' you can do, Child. I'm in God's hands, as we all are. But you never realize it quite so clearly as when you face the grim reaper squarely in the face."

Shelby struggled to hold her own tears in check. She knew Twila had seen her struggle when her friend gave her a gentle smile. "There is one thing you can do for me, Child."

"Anything." Shelby hated feeling useless.

"Let me see you swim in the ocean before I go."

Terror squeezed Shelby's heart, and she felt as though she couldn't catch her breath.

Twila took her hand. "You can do it, Child. I know you can. I just want to be around to see it."

"I–I can't promise," she stuttered.

"Child, I know that. But you can try."

"I can try," Shelby said faintly. Going on the sea had been more than she'd ever imagined she could do; she couldn't imagine actually going into the sea.

"That's all I ask," Twila said. She squeezed Shelby's hand and released it.

Shelby swallowed, then looked around. "Where's Scarlet?"

Twila rose. "Try lookin' overboard," she answered.

"Overboard?" Shelby whirled frantically. "Did anyone see her fall?"

"Fall?" Twila snorted. "That little puffball went over willingly, with Jesse."

Shelby rushed to the rail. The crew was splashing and laughing as they tossed a ball back and forth. Scarlet was in the midst of the fray, dog-paddling for all she was worth.

Shelby watched the fun for a minute. She wished she had the courage to join them. Her T-shirt clung to her damply already. The temperature had to be nearly ninety-five, with humidity that high as well.

"Looks good, doesn't it?" Twila spoke in her ear. "You could just jump right in there with them while I'm standin' here watchin'."

Shelby gasped and looked at the water. It did look rather enticing in this heat. A brilliant blue, its beauty almost hurt her eyes.

"Do it, Shelby," Twila whispered. "You can stay near the ladder for the first time. I'll be here to grab you if you get scared."

She bit her lip. Her heart felt as though it would pound right out of her chest. Lifting her head, she stared into her friend's face. Twila's sickly color convinced her to try. If her friend could face death so bravely, she could jump into that water. It wouldn't hurt her. She took a deep breath. "Jesse!" she called.

He was splashing and laughing about twenty feet from the boat, but he heard her call and swam toward her.

"I'm coming in, but just for a minute," she told him.

His white teeth flashed with the brilliance of his smile. "I'll be right here. Scarlet and I won't let you drown. Climb down the ladder and ease into the water. It won't seem so scary that way."

Shelby nodded. Her heart still thudding like the heavy tick of a clock, she climbed over the side and carefully stepped down the few rungs to the water. When her feet touched the glassy surface, she gasped and almost scurried back up, then Jesse's hands spanned her waist.

"I've got you," he said softly. He eased her into the warm water.

Scarlet yipped excitedly, and Shelby turned to look for her dog. Scarlet's little head bobbed in the blue sea, and terror swept over Shelby at the sight of her tiny dog in the water.

"Let's just swim to the front of the boat and back. That will be enough for the first time." Jesse's deep voice in her ear comforted her. "I'm going to let go of you and swim right here beside you. You can do it."

His confidence bolstered her courage. She struck out with a few faltering strokes and gained confidence. The warm water felt heavenly, and she pushed away all thought of what might lie beneath the surface of that glasslike surface. The rest of the crew treaded water and watched, all offering encouragement.

"You can do it, Shelby!" Heather called.

"Way to go, Child!" Twila called from above her head.

Shelby felt as though each stroke sloughed off a layer of fear. She finally touched the ladder again. The success of her first swim closed her throat with emotion. "I did it!" Jesse's smiling face was close to hers, and she wanted to throw her arms around his neck and kiss him.

"I'm so proud of you," he whispered. He touched her cheek. "Up you go."

With a last glance of gratitude, she scampered up the ladder. "Take care of Scarlet," she called.

"Scarlet and I are buds," Jesse told her. "I won't let anything happen to her. Or to you," he added.

Somehow Shelby knew that was true. She'd faced her fear and found it less terrifying than she'd ever imagined. She wasn't ready to claim total victory yet, but this was a start.

twelve

In spite of their elation over Shelby's swim, the Doldrums left the crew snappish and irritable by evening. The sails hung limp as a dishrag, and the oppressive heat and humidity pressed in on Shelby and left her breathless.

Reluctantly, she went below to the galley to prepare supper. The close confines intensified the heat. She looked through the refrigerator to try to find something that wouldn't have to be cooked.

"How about grilling some fish topside?"

She hadn't heard Jesse come down, and she turned with a start. He wore a grin that lifted her dour spirits.

"A flying fish just landed on deck, and Andy had the presence of mind to grab it before it flipped back into the water. We have a small gas grill in storage. Feel like grilled fish steaks?" He looked like a boy who had just brought his first girlfriend a bouquet of flowers.

Flowers couldn't have pleased Shelby more. "I was just feeling sorry for myself that I had to cook in this pressure cooker."

Jesse's grin widened. "Should I test you to see if you're well done?"

"You've saved me from well done; I'm only rare." Shelby began to gather other items for dinner. There was leftover macaroni salad and tinned fruit, and she could add potatoes in foil to the grill. The crew shouldn't complain about that. She was so lost in thought, she almost missed Jesse's next comment.

"You're a rare one all right," he said softly.

Her breath caught in her throat, and she turned to stare at him with wide eyes. The admiration in his voice seemed genuine. The appreciation in his eyes warmed her but left her tongue-tied. A warm flush stung her cheeks, and she dropped her gaze.

Jesse cleared his throat. "I'll get the grill."

"Meet you on deck," she told him. Her heart was light as she gathered up the rest of the food. On deck, Andy had already finished filleting the fish. She glanced around. "Where's Twila?"

"She was still feeling a little punk," Heather said. "She went to lie down."

She must be feeling awful if she went to that stifling cabin, Shelby speculated. Shelby couldn't imagine sleeping down there tonight, but they would have no choice.

Jesse brought the grill up from the hold. He got it started and shooed her away. "I'll handle the grilling. Even Heather won't complain about my cooking if I stick to grilling."

Heather made a see-saw motion with her hand. "I'll reserve judgment," she said with a grin.

They worked in companionable silence. Shelby was barely conscious of the way Brice bantered with Andy and Heather. She was too aware of Jesse's broad-shouldered figure beside her as he expertly flipped the fish and occasionally poked the potatoes to see if they were done. The mouthwatering aroma of grilled fish made her stomach rumble. It would be good to taste someone else's cooking for a change.

They sat Indian style on the deck and ate their meal. Heather took one bite and declared Jesse the king of the grill. After dinner Jesse got a bucket and brought water up on deck to wash the dishes.

He wouldn't let Shelby help with cleanup. "You need a break," he told her.

Shelby reclined on the deck and watched him out of the corner of her eye. There was an indefinable difference about him tonight. He kept sending her admiring glances and smiles that set her heart racing. Brice sat with his lips tight; he grew more silent as the evening trickled away. His expression baffled and morose, his gaze lingered several times on his brother's face.

Dark fell, and the moon came out, full and golden. Andy and Heather excused themselves and went to bed, but Brice still glowered, though he said little. Shelby wondered if he would refuse to go to bed until Jesse did. She felt half irritated at both of them. She wasn't a bone to be fought over.

Shelby yawned and got to her feet. "I suppose we have to go to bed soon. Our cabins will be miserable."

"I've got the first watch," Jesse said.

"I've got the second," Brice said. "I think I'll turn in." He pointedly waited for Shelby to lead the way to the salon.

Shelby wondered what he would do if she told him she was staying up for awhile. She decided not to test it. She wasn't up to a confrontation tonight.

"Good night," she told Jesse. She tried to be as quiet as possible as she went down the stairs. When she would have gone to her cabin, Brice put a hand on her arm and held her back.

"Don't read anything into the way Jesse was acting tonight," he told her. "I told him how I felt about you, and he disapproves. He thinks I'll hurt you, and he's just trying to prove a point."

Jesse's admiration and thoughtfulness had been a show? She felt as though she'd been hit in the stomach. She'd been looking forward to a pleasant interval of daydreaming before she went to sleep. Pressure built in Shelby's chest, and she wanted to scream at Brice. He'd just ruined a very enjoyable evening. "I don't want to talk about this right now," she said tightly.

The tenderness in his gaze was replaced with uncertainty. "Don't you understand what I'm trying to tell you? I love you, Shelby. I told Jesse I wanted to spend the rest of my life with you."

Shock froze her tongue for a moment. "I–I don't know what to say, Brice," she stammered.

A tiny frown wrinkled his forehead. "I thought you cared for me, Shelby. Was I wrong?"

"I like you very much, Brice, but I'm not sure I'm ready to be more than friends."

His frown deepened. "Let's test it, shall we?"

Before she realized what he intended, he took her in his arms and pressed his lips to hers. Instead of the wild exultation she'd felt when Jesse kissed her, she felt numb. Pity kept her from tearing away at once, but she gently pulled back after a moment.

His eyes darkened, but his fingers still gripped her shoulders. "It's Jesse, isn't it?" he asked with a trace of bitterness. "He's the one who'll break your heart, not me. All Jesse loves is his precious sea. It will never work."

In spite of her own agreement with that view, Shelby's temper flared. "That's for Jesse and me to decide, Brice. I'm sorry if I hurt you, but I never gave you reason to think of me as more than a friend."

As quickly as it had flared, his anger died. "You're right, Shelby. It's not your fault. Can I still hope you'll change your mind?" He dropped his hands to his side.

Shelby reached out and pressed his hand. "Please don't, Brice. I'm afraid it would be useless. I would hate to lose you as a friend."

His smile twisted slightly with pain, but he managed to smile. "You might be my sister-in-law someday, so we'd better be friendly."

Pain flared, and she turned her gaze away. "I doubt that, Brice, but thanks for being so understanding."

He gave a bark of laughter. "Understanding—that's my middle name. It's my lunkhead brother who needs to wake up."

Shelby smiled sadly. "Good night, Brice." She didn't want to talk about it anymore. Her pain needed some space to come to grips with what Brice had told her. Jesse wasn't interested in her; he merely was trying to save his brother from her clutches. It was a bitter pill to swallow. She should be used to it; their relationship had been strewn with the graves of her dead hopes. But no matter how much she tried to guard her heart, Jesse had crept in.

Conscious of Brice's gaze, she hurried to her room before she disgraced herself by bursting into tears. For an evening that had begun so brightly, it had ended with dark edges. Opening the door to her cabin, she slipped inside. Twila's breathing sounded labored, and guilt shamed her.

Her adolescent yearnings after Jesse seemed inane next to
the future her friend faced.

She read her Bible awhile, then prayed for God to be
with Twila. What if Twila didn't survive the trip? She had
to try to convince Twila to tell Jesse. It was only right that
he should know. But ultimately, it was Twila's decision.
She left her shorts and T-shirt on and lay on top of the bed.
She had watch at three A.M.

The cabin was hot and oppressive. She wondered how
Twila was managing to sleep. After tossing and turning for
more than an hour, Shelby got up. She had to have some
air. The boat was silent except for the gentle lap of water
against the hull. The galley was dark, but she knew her
way around by now and managed to get to the deck.

Jesse sat silently in the navigational cabin. His bulk at the
helm gave Shelby a strange sense of peace and safety. He
knew what he was doing, and she didn't have to be afraid.
Except of what his nearness did to her peace of mind, she
amended. Leaning against the railing, she stared out over
the sea. The brilliant moon cast glimmers of gilt over the
waves.

Though she made no noise, Jesse seemed to sense her
presence. The flash of his teeth in the moonlight told her of
his smile. Why shouldn't he smile? He had accomplished
his mission this evening. His actions had pushed his brother
into declaring his love and forced her to repel him.

Jesse stood and stretched. "Couldn't sleep?"

"Too hot." She sat on the seat next to him. "If you could
sleep, I'll take your turn at the helm."

"I'm not sleepy." He nodded toward the clouds drifting
across the face of the moon. "It's getting ready to blow. I'll

have to waken the rest of the crew shortly."

Terror ran through her veins like ice water. "How bad?"

"Likely a pretty stiff gale. We'll try to run before it as the wind freshens." He placed a hand over hers.

She clung to his hand, its warmth pushing back the ice-water terror that had been sent coursing through her. "I thought maybe we were going to escape storms this trip. I've been praying for that."

His smile was gentle, and he squeezed her hand. "If God gave us smooth sailing all the time, we would never face our fear and grow beyond it."

"You're never afraid." She didn't want to let go of his hand, and he showed no inclination to pull it away.

"A man who is never afraid is a fool or an idiot," Jesse said. "But a storm in our life gives us the chance to test ourselves, to go beyond what we thought we were capable of doing, helping us to see God's strength instead. When the waves come, face them, Shelby. Face them and see the hand of God."

"When you put it that way, it sounds almost exciting instead of terrifying," she said shakily.

He leaned forward and brushed the knuckles of his other hand against her chin. "It is," he said softly.

With his breath upon her face and his hand enveloping hers, a pleasant warmth crept through her. He shifted, and his hand slid down around the back of her neck. Pulling her forward, his lips found hers. Tentatively she returned his kiss, but though it was difficult, she held her full emotion in check. She didn't want him to guess how she really felt. After a moment, she pulled back.

He raised one eyebrow. "What's wrong? Was I wrong to

think you might have finally forgiven me? I'm glad you came on this trip, Shelby."

"So you can save your father's resort," she stated flatly. She was thankful for the reminder of why he'd wanted her to come.

"Because I've gotten a chance to see your goodness. You're a remarkable woman, Shelby West."

"If I'm so remarkable, why aren't I good enough for your brother?" she asked. She stood and turned her back to him, wrapping her arms around herself. The clouds were building on the horizon and beginning to cover the moon.

Jesse gave an exasperated sigh. "I never said that. I don't think he's good enough for you. I don't want to see you hurt."

"It's too late."

He was silent for a long moment. When he spoke again, his voice was expressionless. "I see. In that case, I wish you both the very best."

She opened her mouth to tell him it wasn't Brice who had hurt her, when the wind picked up.

Jesse sprang to his feet. "Wake the crew. We'll make a run for it."

Shelby dashed down to the cabins, shouting for Andy and Heather. Brice opened his door almost immediately at her shout. He was fully dressed, and she realized he was probably preparing to take his turn at the helm.

"A storm," she said breathlessly. Her terror was beginning to creep back.

He nodded. Andy and Heather joined them, and the three of them hurried to help Jesse, while Shelby went to check on Twila.

"I'm awake," Twila said when Shelby pushed the door open. "I love storms; I wouldn't miss this one. You go on up, I'll be right there."

Shelby nodded, though it was too dark for Twila to see her. Closing the door behind her, she became aware of movement. The boat was moving. Hope surged in her chest. Maybe they would outrun the storm. The ship rocked as a wave struck it, and she lurched and caught her balance with her hands on the wall. Her heart in her mouth, she hurried topside.

The crew had everything under control. The sails were in place and luffed with wind. Looking over the side, Shelby saw waves building and beginning to toss the boat. She pumped the bilge, then went to find Jesse.

❦

Jesse barked out orders and fought the wheel. The *Jocelyn* responded and began to scud over the waves like a skater over ice. This blow could take them into the lead, if they were able to take advantage of it. He was glad for something that would take his mind off his pain. Shelby's admission that she was already in love with Brice had left him reeling. He'd been a fool to fight his feelings. Twila had tried to tell him, but he'd been too stubborn to listen, too certain he needed to remain aloof until the voyage was over. Now it was too late.

How would he be able to hide his feelings once Shelby married his brother? Maybe now would be a good time to pursue his interest in oceanography. He'd be gone most of the time, and maybe he could get over this love by the next time he saw her. But in his heart, he didn't know if he could ever get over it. He clenched his jaw and forced himself not to look for Shelby.

The storm gained on them, then was upon them. "Ru
up the storm jib!" he shouted to Brice.

The night seemed to last forever. They all fought th
storm with skill and jibs and daring. Twila still looked ill
so Jesse put her on the helm while he helped the crew with
rigging. As the storm worsened, he ordered the crew t
attach lines to their bodies. One particularly bad wav
knocked Heather to the deck, and she began to slide toward
the water. Andy grabbed her line and prevented her from
falling.

Jesse exulted in the wild wind and waves. He was neve
as close to God as he was in the midst of a storm. It wa
just a fingertip of God's power, and he reveled in seeing it
Stopping beside Shelby, he shouted above the wind. "Se
what I meant? Can you feel God?"

Her face was drained of color, except for her green eye
that stared out of her white face. "I'm too scared to look!"
she shouted.

He grinned. "Look for Him, Shelby. Find Him here, and
you'll never fear it again." She smiled gamely, and hi
smile faltered at the surge of love that swept over him.

"I'll try," she said.

He pressed her shoulder and moved along to check on
the rest of the crew.

The storm blew out around dinnertime the next day. By
Jesse's calculations, they were fifteen hundred miles close
to the Horn. "This ill wind has blown us some good," he
told the crew.

"Great. I think I'll go back to bed," Twila remarked.

She didn't look good. Jesse was beginning to worry

about her. He resolved to ask Shelby about her the next chance he had. If he ever had another chance after making such a fool of himself.

Shelby prepared a simple meal of hamburgers and macaroni and cheese for dinner. Jesse was ravenous, as were the rest of the crew. They hadn't eaten for twenty-four hours—the seas had been too rough to allow Shelby to cook. The crew wolfed down the food, then they all went to their beds. Brice took the first watch, since Jesse hadn't been to bed for almost forty-eight hours.

As he crawled into his bed, Jesse thanked the Lord for keeping them all safe. He thought maybe even Shelby had seen a new side of the sea. But she belonged to his brother; it was none of his business.

thirteen

Over the next six weeks Jesse kept his distance. Shelby
kept watching for an opportunity to explain what she had
meant, but he seemed to make sure they were never alone.
And how did a woman go about confessing her love for a
man, anyway? A man who thought she loved his brother.
That brother saw his opportunity and pressed his suit as
well. The crew spent their time playing games, reading,
and performing their duties of reefing sails, making fresh
water, and pumping the bilge.

Twila rallied enough to get out of bed. She went about
her duties, but with a subdued air. Jesse tried to tease her,
but she responded with only the ghost of her former spirit.
To Shelby's eyes, Twila began to fade like an overblown
rose, drooping noticeably as the weeks went by and they
approached the Horn. She prayed daily that Twila would
make it far enough to see her goal.

Twila spent a lot of time sitting on the bow and gazing
off toward Cape Horn. One Sunday, when they were about
two weeks from the Horn, Shelby sank beside her with
Scarlet in tow and handed her a glass of tepid tea. It was a
good time to talk. The rest of the crew were aft playing
checkers. It was too hot to do anything else. At the moment,
the Antarctic sounded wonderful.

Twila took a sip and grimaced. "You make great tea,
Child, but it surely needs ice." Their ice had melted long

ago, and freezer space was too precious to waste on ice.

Shelby smiled, but stared at her worriedly. Twila's skin color was tinged with orange, and even the whites of her eyes were yellowing.

Twila saw her stare and smiled. "I'd make a good Halloween pumpkin, wouldn't I? But I'm not in pain, just tired."

"Have you told Jesse?" Shelby didn't see how Jesse could fail to notice Twila's color. It was becoming too pronounced to miss.

"I'm going to tell all of the crew before bedtime," Twila said with a quiet dignity. "I may not have much time left, but somehow I have to hold on until we reach the Horn."

Shelby didn't reply. She didn't want to discourage her friend, but she doubted they would make it in time.

"What's happened between you and Jesse? He seems to be avoidin' you." Twila took another sip of tea.

Shelby sighed. She didn't want to bother Twila with her problems. "He thinks I'm in love with Brice."

Twila gave a short laugh. "That boy has never been one to give up. Why isn't he fightin' for you?"

"He thinks it's the noble thing—to back out of the picture when his brother is involved."

"How'd he get the harebrained idea you love Brice?"

"He thinks that's what I meant when I told him it was too late to warn me against getting involved. I meant my feelings were involved with him, but he misunderstood. I don't know how to fix it." Shelby pulled her braid over one shoulder and began to replait it.

"He won't take that answer for long. He'll notice that Brice doesn't take you into the moonlight or hover at your elbow. I'm surprised he hasn't picked up on it already."

She shook her head. "The lad is slowin' down."

Shelby tossed her braid to her back again and pulled Scarlet into her lap. A burst of laughter aft echoed toward the bow.

Twila jerked her head toward the sound. "I hate to spoil their enjoyment." She got to her feet. "But it has to be done. I'm not sure I'll be able to get out of bed tomorrow."

Sorrow clutched Shelby's heart, but she bravely got to her feet and followed Twila toward the huddled crew.

Jesse's welcoming smile faded when he saw the expression on Shelby's face. His gaze darted from her to Twila. Concern replaced the bewilderment. "Twila, you don't look well. Heather, have you checked her out today?"

Heather bit her lip. "No, but I will right away." She stood and started toward the hold.

Twila held up a hand. "Don't bother, Heather. It's time I tell all of you what's wrong."

Heather stopped, and all four faces stared at Twila expectantly. Shelby wanted to take the burden from Twila, but it wasn't her place. Twila had to tell them in her own way.

"I have liver cancer," Twila said calmly. "From the looks of my skin and eyes, I'd guess I don't have long, do I, Heather?"

For several long minutes no one spoke. Heather seemed frozen in place, then tears filled her eyes. She dropped her gaze.

The color drained from Jesse's face. He jumped to his feet, shaking his head in a frenzied expression of denial. "I'll change course for the mainland. There will be doctors in Chili. We'll find you help, Twila."

"Child, you are too shocked to be thinkin' to suggest

such a thing. You haven't asked how I know this for certainty or what I want. All the doctors in the world won't change the facts."

Jesse fell silent, but his white face betrayed his shock and grief. "What can I do, Twila?"

"You can get me to Cape Horn," she said. "Then I can go easy. Jesus is waitin' for me, and I'm ready to go as soon as I've seen it."

Jesse spread his hands helplessly. "I'll do the best I can. You hold on, Twila. You have to hold on." He turned to Andy. "Fire up the engines."

Andy's eyes widened, but he didn't argue. He stood and nodded. "We may need to save some fuel in case we get in trouble at the Horn."

"We'll worry about the Horn when we get there. Let's move. Now!"

Jesse's voice brooked no argument. Brice and Andy immediately left to carry out Jesse's instructions.

Shelby knew this would cost him the race. They would arrive with no fuel left, if they arrived at all. Strangely, she felt no fear.

Jesse enfolded Twila in his arms and buried his face in her shoulder. She patted his back as she would a child. "Got any messages for your mama?" she asked. "I'm looking forward to this, Jesse, so don't grieve for me."

"I'm grieving for me," came Jesse's muffled reply. He drew a deep breath and pulled away. His eyes were wet, but he was a strong enough man not to be ashamed of honest tears of love.

Shelby had loved him before, but she felt a new love and admiration for him now. He was a good man, a man worthy of any woman's love. He willingly gave up his dream without a murmur. Not many men would do what he was doing.

"Shelby, would you help me to bed, Child? You, too, Heather. I'm not sure I can make it."

Shelby stepped forward quickly and took her arm. "It's so hot below, Twila. Would you like me to make you a pallet on the deck?"

Twila's dull eyes brightened, and she nodded. "I could look up into God's handiwork through the night," she said. "You're a thoughtful child." She looked to Jesse. "Don't you let her get away, Jesse. She loves you, you know."

Shelby's mouth opened, but no words came. Stricken, she stared at Twila. She was afraid to look at Jesse.

"I won't let her get away," Jesse said.

Shelby dared a glance. Impassive, he stared back with a patient expression as though he was humoring a child. Of course! He thought Twila was confused. Shelby breathed a sigh of relief. She looked away in confusion.

The rumble beneath her feet told her the men had succeeded in starting the motor. Jesse strode toward the navigation cabin. "We're going to get you there, Twila."

Shelby helped Twila sink to the deck, then she and Heather went to the cabin and fetched blankets, a sheet, and a pillow.

"Will we get her there in time?" Shelby asked Heather.

"I don't know," Heather said. "She might make it two weeks, but there's no way of guaranteeing it."

"Is there anything you can do to help her?" Shelby knew the answer before she asked it, but she couldn't still the stab of hope.

Heather shook her head. "Make her comfortable. That's

all we can do. And pray, of course."

"Of course," Shelby echoed.

"You've known about this for awhile, haven't you?" Heather said.

Shelby nodded. "She made me promise not to tell anyone until she was ready."

"I should have seen it," Heather said morosely. "If I hadn't been so sure it was a bug or seasickness. . ."

"It wouldn't have mattered," Shelby told her. "She knew she was dying when she boarded the ship. She wanted to keep her dignity as long as possible."

Heather nodded, but she kept wiping tears as they went back to the deck and made up Twila's pallet. They got Twila settled, with Scarlet curled up beside her, and she fell asleep as soon as her head touched the pillow.

Heather touched Shelby's hand. "Go to Jesse, Shelby. He loves Twila like a mother. This is going to hit him hard."

"I don't know that he would welcome my presence," Shelby said.

"He has no one else." Heather gave her a gentle shove. "Go talk to him."

Reluctantly, Shelby went to find Jesse. She was sure he would send her away.

He glanced up briefly when she sat beside him. "Why didn't you tell me?" His voice was tight with anger and grief.

In a flash, Shelby realized he had to blame someone right now, and she was the only target. She didn't try to defend herself. "I'm sorry," she said.

Jesse pounded the wheel. "I should have seen it! What kind of a man am I that someone I love could be that sick and yet I didn't see it?"

His self-loathing filled Shelby with tender pity. She reached over and took his hand. It was cold and rough with calluses from tugging on the ropes. "You can't fix everything, Jesse. You've told me several times to trust God and not be afraid. Now you need to practice what you preach."

"This is Twila's life we're talking about, not some irrational fear," he said hotly. "She's going to die, Shelby." His hands shook, and he clutched the wheel as though he was afraid that every solid thing around him might vanish.

Shelby knew she should be angered at his thoughtless dismissal of her fear, but again, she knew he was just lashing out. She nodded gently. "Yes, she is, Jesse. But then so are you, and so am I."

He fell silent, then nodded. A wry grin flickered across his face then disappeared. "You can preach pretty good yourself, Miss West."

Shelby smiled and pressed his hand. His fingers curled around hers, and he raised them to his lips. Her heart sped up, but she stared steadfastly into his eyes.

"My brother will have my hide," Jesse said. He dropped her hand and busied himself with the instruments. "You'd better go check on Twila."

Dismissed again. Every time she felt they had moved one step closer, he stepped sideways. She wanted to clear the air between them, but this was not the time. Their focus had to stay on Twila. There would be time to settle other issues later. She hid her sigh and got to her feet. "Good night."

"Good night." He looked up briefly from his scrutiny of the gauges. "Thanks, Shelby."

"I didn't do anything," she said.

"You were there and hauled me back to shore."

She forced a smile. "Good night."

He went back to his gauges, and she went to Twila.

❦

The boat skimmed across the waves like a ballet dancer across the dance floor. Jesse checked his navigational equipment often, and he paced the deck whenever he wasn't with Twila or manning the helm. Twila grew weaker daily, and her color became more orange. The whites of her eyes turned pure yellow. Her periods of wakefulness were shorter and shorter. Shelby began to fear they wouldn't make it in time, but somehow Twila clung to life.

The winds grew colder, but Twila refused to go below. Jesse made a makeshift shelter, and Shelby piled blankets on top of her. At night, all of the crew brought their blankets up on deck and curled up to sleep next to Twila to keep her warm.

About ten days after Twila told the crew about her condition, the morning held a new crispness. Jesse shook Twila gently. "Twila, we're almost there." His voice was filled with a suppressed excitement.

Rubbing the sleep from her eyes, Shelby sat up and propped up Twila with several pillows.

Twila visibly fought to cling to consciousness. "We're there?" she murmured.

"Almost," Jesse said. "And it's clear. We should be able to see it pretty soon."

Shelby felt a bittersweet sense of victory and loss mingled together. She had made it herself, but that fact paled in comparison to seeing the finish line arriving for Twila. If she could just hang on a few hours more. Staring across the deck at her friend, she didn't see how she had managed to hold on this long. She prayed God would be gracious and give Twila these next few hours.

fourteen

The *Jocelyn* danced across the waves toward their destination. The weather had been remarkably fair, though cold. The temperature dipped so low that they had no choice but to carry Twila to the cabin. Her dusky skin was like yellow-brown parchment now, thin and fragile. She barely protested at the move, too sick to raise much objection.

Their navigation equipment indicated they would see Cape Horn today. Shelby bundled Twila up as warmly as she could, and as soon as the sun had warmed the air a bit, Jesse carried Twila up to the deck. Gray clouds hung low in the sky.

Jesse glanced worriedly at the clouds. "No sign of williwas," he said. "But they can come screaming out of the sky with practically no warning."

Shelby had heard about the williwas—near hurricane-force winds that whistled off the Horn. She shivered and stared at the sky uneasily.

Twila rallied a bit with the cold air. She sat in a deck chair with quilts bundled around her and stared at the rough seas. "Not as bad as I expected," she said. She almost sounded disappointed.

"We're not there yet, and we're still in the Southern Ocean," Jesse reminded her.

"If the weather holds, do you think we could go ashore

on Cape Horn?" Twila asked wistfully.

Fear clutched Shelby's belly, but she looked to Jesse for the answer. She wouldn't be the one to deny Twila anything at this point.

He nodded. "If the weather holds, we'll take the dinghy." He glanced to Shelby, an apology in his eyes. "You can stay behind if you like, Shelby."

She shook her head. "I'm going, too. I'm not going to be afraid."

"That's right, no need to fear, Child. What's the worst thing that can happen? You can't scare me with heaven." Having said her piece, Twila leaned her head back against the chair and closed her eyes.

The boat rode the swells with grace and determination. Shelby strained her eyes to see the rocky shoreline of Cape Horn. The gray fog rolled across the seas then suddenly broke.

"There it is, Twila!" Jesse leaned down and supported Twila with his strong arm.

She opened her eyes and strained to see. "I see it!" Her exclamation was a mere whisper, but her black eyes were bright and aware. "Oh, Jesse, I see it!" Tears welled in her eyes. "Praise be to God, He allowed me to see Cape Horn."

"Thank You, Father," Jesse agreed.

His eyes were wet, and Shelby could barely see through the film of tears moistening her own eyes. She took Twila's hand, and the rest of the crew gathered around and exclaimed in awe.

"Do we dare try to make a landing, Jesse?" Brice asked. "What about the race?"

Twila's eyes brightened, but she didn't plead with words.

The hope in her eyes caused Shelby to add her pleading gaze to Twila's.

Jesse nodded. "Inflate the dinghy. We're going ashore."

Heather and Andy whooped with delight. The fact that they were all willingly abandoning their dream of winning the race didn't seem to bother any of them. No sacrifice was too great for Twila. Within minutes, Andy and Brice had inflated the dinghy. Jesse maneuvered the boat closer to shore, and they dropped anchor. The excitement had rallied Twila, and she even managed to climb into the dingy with only a little help from Jesse.

The waves were large, but Shelby found that her fear lessened with watching the wonder on Twila's face. The dinghy touched the shore, then Jesse jumped out and pulled it to dry land. Reaching in, he lifted Twila into his arms and stepped onto the granite shore of Cape Horn. Cliffs of granite covered with peat and evergreen thickets rose before them. Misty fog rolled over the rocks, and Shelby shivered from the cold, forbidding terrain.

They stayed only a few minutes, just long enough for Twila to see the Cape Horn monument to the sailors who had died off this rocky point. Twila's sudden burst of strength waned, and Jesse hurried to get her safely aboard the *Jocelyn*. By the time they reached the boat, Twila was too weak to help them much, and it was only with difficulty that Jesse and Brice managed to get her aboard.

The wind freshened, and the clouds grew black. "Let's get out of here!" Jesse shouted. The men sprang to work, while Heather and Shelby half carried Twila to the cabin. Within minutes the wind was screaming and waves began to batter the boat. Shelby strapped Twila to the bed, then she and Heather sat and each held one of Twila's hands.

Shelby tore her gaze from her friend's face. "She's going now, isn't she?" she whispered. There was no mistaking that odd rattle Twila's breathing made.

Heather nodded slowly. "I think so. Jesse would want to be here. I'll have Andy take his place."

"I can do it," Shelby offered.

"No, Twila wants you here."

Indeed, Twila's fingers clutched Shelby's hand. With the boat lolling in the massive waves, Heather clung to the wall and made her way as best she could from the room.

Shelby smoothed the black hair from Twila's face and sang a verse of "O That Will Be Glory." A half-smile drifted across Twila's face, and she gave a contented smile.

Jesse burst into the room, his eyes wild with grief. He knelt beside Shelby at the side of Twila's bed and took her hand. "I'm here, Twila."

She opened her eyes with obvious difficulty. "That's good, Jesse. You take care of this child, you hear?"

"I hear."

"You know Shelby loves you, don't you, Jesse?" Twila's eyes were becoming unfocused.

"He does now that you told him for me," Shelby said with a smile. She heard Jesse's intake of breath but didn't dare look at him. At least the secret was out in the open.

"And Jesse loves you, Shelby."

"That's right," Jesse said in a voice thick with emotion.

This time it was Shelby's turn to jerk with surprise.

"Take her hand, Jesse," Twila instructed insistently.

Jesse gripped Shelby's hand with cold fingers. Shelby finally dared to turn and meet his gaze, catching her breath at the love she saw shining in his eyes.

"I want to hear you ask her," Twila said in a fading voice.

Shelby was confused for a moment, then Jesse's deep voice drove all thought from her mind.

"Shelby West, will you marry me?" His smile was warm and tender.

For a moment Shelby wondered if he was merely placating Twila, but the adoration in his smile banished that fear. "Yes," she breathed.

A tiny sigh escaped Twila's lips. "That's good," she breathed. Then her eyes widened in surprise and joy. "Jesus!" she exclaimed. She tried to sit up but slumped back against the pillows. Her remaining breath leaked from her lips.

"She's gone," Jesse choked. He reached a trembling hand to Twila's face and closed her eyes.

Shelby turned and hid her face in his chest. Sobs shook her, and Jesse buried his face in her hair. They wept together for several minutes. Gradually she became aware that the pitching of the ship had worsened dramatically.

"I'd better get to the bridge," Jesse said. He pressed a kiss to her temple. "We'll talk when this crisis is over."

"I'll come with you."

Jesse shook his head. "It's going to be bad, Shelby. I'm going to send Heather below, too. If you can bear it, wrap Twila in a sheet for a burial at sea. Once we're out of this storm, we'll have a service for her." He gave her a quick kiss then was gone.

Shelby felt she'd been on a roller coaster of grief and joy. They'd lost their friend, but Jesse loved her. She couldn't believe either fact.

Heather entered the cabin in a burst of cold air and the smell of cold sea water. Her face was white with strain. "I've never seen seas like this," she said. "One wave was easily fifty feet tall."

The boat shuddered with another wave, and the force flung them both to the floor. Then the real battering began. Most of the time Shelby didn't know which way was up. She was bruised from being tossed around the cabin, but she was more worried about the men on the deck. She crawled along the floor to the galley.

Heather shouted something at her, but the roar of the wind and waves was too loud to hear her words. Heather began to crawl after her. They reached the galley. Water poured from above, then the men tumbled down.

Jesse crawled to Shelby. "We just have to ride it out," Jesse panted in her ear. "I've reefed the main, and the storm jib is up. All we can do is pray."

Instead of the words bringing terror, Shelby burrowed into Jesse's arms and sighed. She was content with what God would bring. If they followed Twila to heaven, that was fine with her.

The storm raged through the day and all through the night. The crew spent the time lashed and bundled into the rough weather bunks. It was too stormy for them to eat or drink anything; all they could do was ride the waves. Scarlet hunkered in the bunk with Shelby, but she didn't seem as fearful as Shelby was afraid she would be.

The wild night finally ended. When the sun pierced Shelby's closed eyes from the porthole above her head, she groaned, then she realized the wild tossing was over. They had survived the storm. She managed to untangle herself from the blankets and extricated herself from the bunk. She dropped Scarlet to the floor near her litter box, and poked Heather as she passed. The men apparently were on deck.

Heather muttered, then opened her eyes. "I'm awake, I'm awake."

Shelby stumbled weakly to the doghouse. Jesse was at the helm, and his welcoming smile warmed her insides better than a cup of hot coffee could.

"We're alive," she said faintly.

"I was proud of you," Jesse said. He pulled her onto his lap and nuzzled his face in her hair.

Shelby clung to him. "We've lost the race."

He shrugged. "Maybe, maybe not. We're making a run for it as soon as we bury Twila. But whichever way it goes, we're trusting God with this. I learned that much in the last few days."

Shelby chuckled. "But you don't need to win the race. You got me around the Horn. Your insurance will pay off."

Jesse lifted his head. "That was never the real reason," he said. "Somehow I knew I couldn't let you get away. I always wanted an Amazon wife to share my adventures."

Shelby laughed and kissed him. "I never knew what a penchant I have for adventurers," she said. "Or rather, one adventurer in particular."

"Break it up, you two. We have work to do," Andy said, coming up behind them. His sandy beard didn't hide his wide grin.

Jesse released Shelby reluctantly. "We'll talk more later," he promised.

They had a brief, loving burial service for Twila. Jesse

wanted to commit her body to the waves as near the Horn as possible. Heather and Andy sang a duet, and Jesse raised the American flag. Watching the sheet-clad form slip into the water was difficult for Shelby, but somehow it seemed right. It was what Twila had wanted.

"Now let's do our best to win this race—for Twila," Jesse said at the end of the burial.

The crew cheered weakly and raced to hoist the sails. The wind filled the sails, and the *Jocelyn* picked up speed and raced toward their destination. The crew could almost read one another's mind after the long voyage and worked almost as one person. Only one boat was ahead of them.

Jesse used the binoculars and studied his opponent. "It's Palmer." The firm line of lips and the twitch of his jaw betrayed his anger.

Andy nodded. "Good. Makes our win more meaningful."

The wind died just as they thought they might overtake Palmer. His white sails faded into the horizon, and with them, Shelby's burgeoning hope that they might actually win. Not that it mattered for the money. She had enough for both of them now, but she knew Jesse would expect to provide for his wife, not the other way around.

"Start the engines," Jesse ordered.

Shelby knew it was a desperate move. There was little fuel left. And if the boats tied, Palmer would win if he had more fuel left. But they had no choice. Everything hung on the next few hours. Andy ran to start the engines. A minute later the engines rumbled beneath their feet, and *Jocelyn* surged forward.

The boat gained on Palmer's boat. They were near enough now to see the figures onboard. Then the engines died. The *Jocelyn* was out of fuel. Jesse's shoulders sagged in defeat. But a fluttering sound drew their attention. The wind was filling the sails again. The boat responded and sprang forward.

Palmer's angry voice carried over the waves as they drew abreast to his boat, *Raptor*.

"More speed, I need more speed!" Palmer screamed. "Start the engines!"

The crew member hurrying to obey caught his foot on a loop of rope and fell. A gust of wind hourglassed Raptor's spinnaker, and Palmer's boat fell behind. His angry voice faded as *Jocelyn* pulled ahead farther and farther. The crew cheered.

But their elation was short-lived. Palmer's crew had managed to start their engines, and Raptor soon drew abreast of them. They were still struggling with the spinnaker, so engine power was all that pushed Palmer's boat. Neck and neck the boats raced toward the waiting crowds at the dock. Welcoming banners flew in the wind, and Shelby prayed with every ounce of her being that they would be the ones to reach the finish line first. The *Jocelyn* raced toward the judges' boats, but *Raptor* kept pace.

Ten feet from the finish, *Raptor*'s engines sputtered and died. Palmer was out of fuel, but the crew had fixed their problems with the spinnaker. The two boats hurtled toward the finish. Shelby couldn't tell who was the winner. It would be the judges' decision.

"Drop anchor!" Jesse hurried to help Andy and Brice drop the sails.

The suspense tightened Shelby's chest as they waited for the judge to announce a winner. A flashbulb had gone off as they passed the nearest judge's boat, and they were probably waiting to see what the photo revealed. The judges conferred, then one of them stepped forward with a megaphone.

"According to our finish photo, the judges have determined *Jocelyn* to have won the Southern Cup race. Both crews are to be commended. Please come ashore for the prize awards."

Jocelyn's crew erupted into cheers. Jesse swung Shelby into the air, then pulled her close and hugged her. Tears sprang to Shelby's eyes. They'd done it! Or rather, God had done it. Only His hand could have accomplished this. Gratitude filled her heart.

They pulled into port and docked near the welcoming banners. Crowds cheered, and Shelby shivered with excitement. Jesse stood with his arm around Shelby as they docked.

"Somehow this doesn't mean what I thought it would," he whispered into her hair. "The real prize was won when you said you'd marry me."

Shelby leaned her head against his chest. Her heart was near to overflowing with happiness. "Your dad's resort is saved," she reminded him. "And there will be enough money to fix it up, make it a real tourist draw. We can pay for a complete renovation. New carpet and everything."

Jesse tipped her gaze up to meet his. "You'd be willing to use some of our money to do that?" he asked. His dark eyes were tender and adoring.

His assumption that his money was hers, too, and that she had some say in how it would be spent warmed her. Jesse was a rare man. She kissed him. "Let's go get our prize," she said.

They stepped ashore and accepted the congratulations of

the crowd. They had to wait for Palmer and his crew to join them.

Palmer's face was dark with rage. "You've got it all, don't you, Titus?" He pushed spectators away and accepted his second-place prize without grace.

Shelby felt sorry for him in spite of his bad manners. She didn't care about the money. God have given her all that she really needed. Palmer needed to seek God's face for true happiness, she realized. She hoped the opportunity would come to share God's love with him. It was what her uncle would want, too, she knew.

Jesse accepted the prize money of two hundred thousand dollars. It was nearly dark by the time the photo shoot was over, and the congratulatory crowds had dissipated. Jesse kept his arm draped around Shelby's shoulders as they walked back to the dock for their things. They would sleep in the hotel tonight, but they needed clean clothes.

They agreed to meet on deck in fifteen minutes. Shelby rummaged through the sea chest for clean clothes. Her fingers accidentally pressed against the side of the chest, and a spot popped out. A hiding place? She lifted the rest of the chest's contents out of the way and peered into the compartment. An envelope with strong, slanted writing lay there. It had her name on it.

Her mouth dropped open, and she reached in with cold fingers to take it. She opened the sealed envelope and pulled out the single sheet of paper.

Shelby,
   So you've found my old sea chest and have been curious enough to look through it. I knew you would.

*You struck me as an enterprising young woman. I
suppose you're wondering why I made you my beneficiary. It was the only way I could think of to cure
you of your fear of water. With that kind of fear, only
a strong incentive would force you to confront it. You
and your mom have had a hard life, and I could have
merely left money to you to take care of her, but
I wanted to do more than help you financially. I
wanted to make you face yourself and test God's
provision for you. And I wanted Jesse to have a reason to be around you, too. Call me a meddling old
man, but I hoped a romance might blossom between
the two of you. That would please me. If not, I
hope you are a stronger woman for facing your
fear. I know you will use the money wisely and for
God's glory.*

*Your loving uncle,
Lloyd*

Shelby blinked back tears. What a sweet man. She hoped
he knew that his dreams had been realized. Holding the
note, she went to find Jesse.

He read the note in silence, then stared at her with a tender gaze. "I hope he knows somehow."

"I think he just might." She reached up and kissed him.

Jesse reached into his pocket. "I have something for you.
I've carried it with me for years, hoping to give it to the
woman I wanted to marry someday." He held out a tiny
ruby-encrusted spyglass, too small for real use. "My dad
used to search for sunken ships when he was young. He
found it on a sunken ship off the coast of Florida and gave

it to my mother. It's a reminder to keep watch for the real treasures of life."

Shelby took the spyglass with trembling fingers. It felt warm from Jesse's hand. Her throat was too tight with love to speak.

"Look through it," he urged.

She raised it to her eye. "A kaleidoscope," she gasped. The rainbow of colors dazzled her eyes.

"Sometimes true beauty is hidden," Jesse said soberly. "But I saw yours from the first moment we met. Are you sure you're up to living with an adventurer?"

"I'm sure," Shelby said. She'd longed for adventure, and now she'd found it. An adventure that would last a lifetime together.

"There's just one more thing," Jesse said, picking up Scarlet from the floor. "No more hair bows for Scarlet."

Shelby smiled and tucked her arm into Jesse's. "As long as you allow bows for our daughter."

"I think Scarlet would agree with that," Jesse said as he took her in his arms.

A Letter To Our Readers

Dear Reader:

In order that we might better contribute to your reading enjoyment, we would appreciate your taking a few minutes to respond to the following questions. We welcome your comments and read each form and letter we receive. When completed, please return to the following:

Rebecca Germany, Fiction Editor
Heartsong Presents
PO Box 719
Uhrichsville, Ohio 44683

1. Did you enjoy reading *Love Ahoy* by Colleen Coble?
   ❑ Very much! I would like to see more books
     by this author!
   ❑ Moderately. I would have enjoyed it more if

   _____

   _____

   _____

2. Are you a member of **Heartsong Presents**? Yes ❑ No ❑
   If no, where did you purchase this book?_____

   _____

3. How would you rate, on a scale from 1 (poor) to 5 (superior), the cover design?_____

4. On a scale from 1 (poor) to 10 (superior), please rate the following elements.

   _____ Heroine   _____ Plot

   _____ Hero   _____ Inspirational theme

   _____ Setting   _____ Secondary characters

5. These characters were special because_____

_____

_____

6. How has this book inspired your life?_____

_____

_____

7. What settings would you like to see covered in future
   Heartsong Presents books?_____

_____

_____

8. What are some inspirational themes you would like to see
   treated in future books?_____

_____

_____

9. Would you be interested in reading other **Heartsong
   Presents** titles?   Yes ❑   No ❑

10. Please check your age range:
     ❑ Under 18   ❑ 18-24   ❑ 25-34
     ❑ 35-45   ❑ 46-55   ❑ Over 55

Name _____

Occupation _____

Address _____

City _____ State _____ Zip _____

Email _____

TAILS
of LOVE

Matchmakers come in all shapes and sizes. And in the case of these four romantic adventures, the little connivers come with tails. They'll dig in their paws and claws and stop at nothing until their owners are happily leashed in wedded bliss.

This collection contains fur-flying fun that will make you appreciate your own pets' intuitive interaction with their humans. You'll thank God again and again for four-footed blessings.

paperback, 352 pages, 5 ³⁄₁₆" x 8"

♥ ● ♥ ● ♥ ● ♥ ● ♥ ● ♥ ❤ ♥ ● ♥ ● ♥ ● ♥ ● ♥ ● ♥

♥ ● ♥ ● ♥ ● ♥ ● ♥ ● ♥ ❤ ♥ ● ♥ ● ♥ ● ♥ ● ♥ ● ♥

······Presents······